THE SUMMER O

Simon Burt was born
in North Kensington, London.

Two of his stories appeared in the Faber collection of
lesbian and gay writing, *Mae West is Dead*, and he has
had short fiction published in the *New Statesman*, *Cosmo-
politan* and *Fiction Magazine*. His collection *Floral Street*
received great praise from the critics and was acclaimed
in the *New York Native* as 'Taut, tightly written ... A
collection of stories that leaves one eager for more'.

The Summer of the White Peacock is his first novel.

by the same author

FLORAL STREET

THE SUMMER OF THE WHITE PEACOCK

Simon Burt

faber and faber

LONDON · BOSTON

First published in 1989
by Faber and Faber Limited
3 Queen Square London WC1N 3AU
This paperback edition first published in 1990

Phototypeset by Input Typesetting Ltd
London SW19 8DR

Printed in Great Britain by
Richard Clay Ltd Bungay Suffolk

© Simon Burt, 1989

A CIP record for this book
is available from the British Library

ISBN 0–571–14217–6

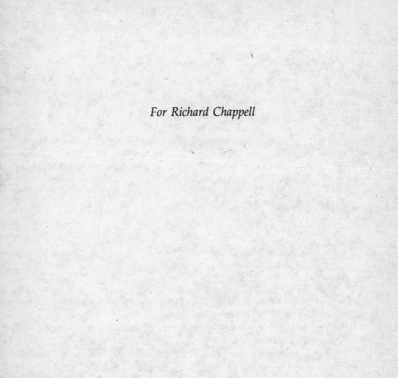

For Richard Chappell

Item, two lips, indifferent red;
item, two grey eyes, with lids to them;
item, one neck, one chin, and so forth.

Twelfth Night

ONE

That was the summer I was going to be the new James Dean.

Seen in the right light, you see, and with a hefty dash of good will, I look like him. Well, a cross between him and Michael Sarrazin actually, with a distinct lean in the Sarrazin direction. Especially that look of something hunted behind the eyes – my eyes, incidentally, give me a lot of trouble: they are very large and very dry and I have to use drops all the time to keep them moist – but that wasn't the look I wanted at all.

I'd had that look. I didn't want to look beach-boy and sun-dappled and wide open and reproachful. That look wasn't getting me anywhere.

I wanted to look unhealthy and inner-city and dangerous. I wanted to look vulnerable and fuck-you at the same time.

So I placed my lights carefully and had my hair cut. Goodbye to the seventies, I thought as I watched the curls falls. I spent hours, and a great deal of money, spiking it and straightening it and brushing it up from my forehead at the right petulant and careless angle.

I had a lot of trouble with the back. It stuck up in all the wrong places. I was for ever smoothing it down. And it revealed my ears, which took a bit of getting used to, because, frankly, the less said about my ears the better.

I hunched my shoulders and smouldered. I narrowed my Sarrazin eyes into a slit-lidded scowl. I went to the gym every morning and tortured myself into sharpening up my torso and losing a stone. I have trouble with my weight. I eat too much. I eat, in fact, most of the time unless I take myself in hand. I went swimming every evening.

And the end result of all this was success. Even if I didn't look too much like James Dean, I looked pretty good. And I was in damn good shape, which is half the battle, and more than can be said for James Dean every now and again. In some of those photographs he looks pretty baggy.

It wasn't as if I didn't have the time. I was out of work. I'd not had even the sniff of an audition since last March, and the less said about last March's audition the better. They didn't want a Michael Sarrazin either. Among other things.

Luckily, I was all right for money, having done a series of fresh-faced and ingenuous coffee advertisements in January that were still paying the rent and keeping me more or less off the streets.

But I was bored. Oh my God, I was bored. Try as you may, you can't spend the whole day in the gym, at the pool, in front of the mirror. There are still desert hours to be filled.

Some of them I spent sunbathing in Holland Park. And the rest I spent sunbathing on my balcony overlooking Holland Park. Overlooking but not overlooked, which meant that although I went on feeling alone, at least I could tan my ass, and that was nice, because whatever they say, and they say quite a lot, about the flash of snow-white buns between honey-baked torso and thigh, I am here to tell you that a matching biscuit-coloured bum is a hundred per cent sexier.

None too easy to acquire, though. Even if you are lucky enough to have, as I have, a drop of indeterminate foreign dusky blood and a non-overlooked suntrap for a balcony, you can only do it for a short while, at least to begin with, because round that particular girdle a little sunshine goes a long way. I overdid it on the first day and I was raw for a week. And that is an uncomfortable – and unwinning – place to be raw. Although, oddly, the resulting funny walk rather helped the James Dean image than otherwise.

But the foreign blood won through in the end and soon I could lie all day in the sun and get darker and darker and no hard feelings. No feelings at all really.

4

The evenings were the worst.

If you've spent all day doing the things most people do after they've finished work, what do you do when the people you could be visiting – if you wanted to visit them, but that's another matter – are doing the things you spent the day doing?

You read. You play games with the sound system. You watch whatever programmes on the television you can bear to watch, which at that time of year is damn near none: the average age of the average television viewer clearly halves in the summer. You treat yourself to the latest video, a film you saw when it first came out and now you can see the seams somehow. You telephone people, none of whom are in, because they're all out doing et cetera, and you run out of witty things to say to their answering machine. You try not to eat.

I thought of taking up tennis. When I was young my symbol of aloneness was a see-saw, because I always wanted to play on one, but there was never anyone around for the other end. Now it's a tennis racket. I managed to arrange one game that whole summer, and that was with my agent, and ended in a bitter squabble about why wasn't I getting any work, a state of affairs each blamed on the other. Slam down the racket. Stalk off the court. Fuck you!

And when the people I called were in, all they could talk about was this marvellous new job they'd landed, six weeks in the Philippines, and what are you doing? After a while I stopped calling and there they were, the desert hours, waiting to be filled.

I took to hanging around bars. A desperate recourse, because if you hang around bars all you meet is the sort of person who likes hanging round bars. And every night I swore it would be only orange juice. And every night it was orange juice for the first half hour, and vodka and orange juice till closing time, and more vodka, and pills, and poppers, at a certain club that shall remain nameless behind Earls Court till three in the morning.

Come to think of it, I can see no reason why the club should remain nameless. It was called – God help us – the Stagecoach, and it was in a side-street off a side-street off Warwick Road. It was called the Stagecoach because it opened on the crest of the Urban Cowboy wave, when we all ambled about in Levi's and check shirts over white vests and agonizing boots. Since then, of course, fashion had moved on, and every night we stood around the redneck fitments of the Stagecoach looking like urban guerrillas.

The club was based on the American model. In America people are fast and loose and cool and talk to one another. At the Stagecoach we couldn't manage that. We stood around. We jammed our thumbs in our webbing belts. We sucked our beer straight from the can. All too James Dean for words. And we were admired. The uninhibited shot pool.

I danced. By myself. It was fun. Sometimes I danced so hard and got so hot I took off my shirt and danced some more. Exciting stuff. But after a while you need a partner. I mean, Narcissus danced. But did he play tennis, or bounce up and down on a see-saw?

At three o'clock I'd walk home, slink about my flat with what I hoped was pantherine tread, until I finally plucked up courage to go to bed. Meanwhile, I thought, my youth and my money are vanishing. Oh yes. I know. It's a familiar story. I shouldn't go on about it.

Then I broke my foot. And a squalid little episode that was.

I was walking home one morning from the Stagecoach through Holland Walk and I was beaten up. I can't even say that I was mugged, because they were clearly not out for money. What they wanted was fear, my fear, and I sure as hell gave them plenty of that.

I was tired. I'd been dancing at the Stagecoach. I was drunk, my ears were singing, my head was aching. My reactions were not of the quickest. I saw a group of what they call youths heading towards me and I thought, Uh-oh, someone's in for it. It didn't occur to me that it was going to be me.

They were singing. I kept on walking and kept my eyes on the ground. It didn't occur to me that it was going to be me until they stopped singing, spread out in a line, and blocked the path.

I still kept on walking. There didn't seem by now to be any alternative. They didn't move. I walked up to one, and was just going to nod and try to slip by when he stopped me with a hand on my chest and the others moved so that I was surrounded. Nobody said anything. Not me, because by now I was scared shitless. Not them, because I guess they felt their body language was eloquent enough.

They pushed me from one to the other round the circle, each push a little harder than the last, until they were frankly punching me one to the other. I was too scared to do anything but be punched. Then I was pushed to the ground. I snapped out of my panic half-way down and saw my chance.

They must all have shifted when I fell, to move closer, to put the boot in, or whatever. I only saw the one in front of my face. Like I said, I'd been spending a lot of time in the gym. I was in good shape. I landed on my front and was up on my hands and toes in the time it took him to lift his foot. I shot like a bullet between his legs, knocked him over and raced away.

They ran after me, but I would have escaped if I hadn't tripped and fallen. I picked myself up, but they were on me again and pushed me up against the wall. I found my tongue at last. All I could think of to say was, Not my face! Not my face! So I shouted that and they all laughed.

The one I'd knocked over arrived after the rest. His nose was bleeding. He stood in front of me.

You hurt me, he said.

Not my face! I shouted.

You fucking hurt me! he said.

Not my face!

So what's so special about your fucking face then? he said. Let's have a look at it, darling.

He struck a match and held it about a millimetre from my eyes. My head was already as far back against the wall as it would go.

Christ! he said. It's that coffee bloke from the telly.

7

The match went out.

Well, he said as he lit another. If we haven't got a famous one. Come on, darling. Let's have another look at your pretty face.

He held the match right up to my eyes again.

OK, he said. Piss off, you lot. This one's mine.

The others fell slowly back against the opposite wall. He put his forearm across my throat and leaned on it.

I said Piss off, he said over his shoulder. Find someone else. This one's got a private lesson to learn.

They pissed off.

Right then, he said. Let's get you into the light. I like to see what I'm doing.

He pinioned me against the wall with his body, and with the arm that wasn't crushing my throat he punched me in the stomach. I nearly threw up. He grabbed both my arms and marched me off to the streetlight. I could only just breathe. He held me up against the lamp-post.

You're not going to run away, are you? he said.

He put his foot on my foot and trod on it. He brought his face up to mine and increased the pressure on my foot so that I opened my mouth to cry out. He ground his open mouth against mine and made, as they say, his first mistake.

He thrust his tongue into my mouth and I bit it. I ground it between my teeth, and he would have howled if he could. As it was, he made a high-pitched squealing noise, and did some grinding of his own. With his foot on mine.

Then he punched me in the gut again. I let go his tongue and he fell off my foot. And I ran. You shouldn't, they reminded me the next day, run on a broken foot, but they weren't there. I didn't look back. I don't know if he followed me. If he did I beat him.

Next morning I woke from a pill-sodden sleep to a foot the size and colour of a beach ball. I only hoped his tongue was in the same condition. I went to the hospital and they strapped it up.

Two broken toes. Not much, considering. But enough, they insisted, to immobilize me for a fortnight. No more gym. No more swimming. No more pantherine slinking. No more dancing, alone or otherwise. Just stay off that foot. If you must walk, walk only on the heel, and use a stick. Dead sexy. Dead James Dean.

I took to my balcony. I lay all day in the sun. I went mahogany from head to toe. One set of toes anyway. If I thought I'd been bored before, I soon found out my mistake. I explored Himalayas of tedium that made me thrash about on my blanket. I was so bored I thought I would die, and frankly looked forward to the prospect, until I was beyond looking forward or backward or anywhere but up into the sky.

Hour after hour I lay naked on my balcony, while what was left of my mind achieved a sort of qualified neutral. I say qualified because beneath the fact that the sun, the pain in my foot, the boredom, my almost rape, all combined into a distant vortex – beneath that there pulsed a vestigial but pervading horror. Time vanished and I barely, but for the horror, existed. I moved, somehow, from balcony to bed and back again as night followed day and night and day. I ate nothing. I have a murky memory of plunging my face into a sinkful of ice-cubes, so I guess I drank. I must have done or I'd have burned up, so someone must have been in control somewhere. It just wasn't me. I didn't know who I was. Or where I was. Only that every now and again there beat up from the pulse of horror something, a state, a noise, that I was later able to analyse into the cry of peacocks from the park.

Or a peacock. A desolate squawking wail that punctuated my trance until I wasn't sure whether it was crying or not, whether I was crying or not. My one sensation a continuous, solitary crark. It was not nice. I wouldn't wish it on my worst enemy. Except maybe the bastard whose tongue I'd gnawed. I sure as hell hoped he was suffering.

My beard grew. I could feel it growing.

The telephone rang and I couldn't answer it. I simply couldn't move.

But the ringing broke the spell. Unless I was coming round anyway. By degrees I was aware. I felt the sun-sodden torpor fall away. The horror drained off me like bathwater when you've pulled the plug and are too lazy to get out of the tub.

I realized I was hungry. Without knowing it I moved. One moment I was on the balcony, the next I was standing in front of a fridge, empty but for a carton of orange juice.

I drank the orange juice.

I had a bath with my foot hung over the edge – which you have to have done before you can appreciate how much of the pleasure it took away. But it still felt good. I left the water filthy. You wouldn't believe how dirty you can get, stark naked on a London balcony.

So I had a shower as well, my foot stuck out beyond the curtain, and washed my hair. Thank the Lord for James Dean. I pushed my hair back from my forehead and felt quite human again.

I scowled into the mirror and decided to keep my beard. I was so much browner there'd probably be a tide-mark if I shaved it off. My foot was a lot easier to walk on. I decided to go and buy something to eat and unstrap it and inspect the damage when I got back.

The telephone rang again just after I'd shut the flat door, but by the time I'd opened up again and hopped through to the bedroom to answer it, whoever was calling had rung off. I went out and bought a mountain of groceries and a newspaper. The date on the newspaper was the fifteenth of June. Ten days till my birthday. And three days since my little incident in Holland Walk. Maybe his tongue was going down too by now.

I went back to the flat and made myself bacon and eggs and a flagon of black, black coffee.

I unstrapped my foot which proved to be a lot less swollen, if no less varicoloured. I sponged it with surgical spirit to get rid of the grime, but I couldn't walk on it unstrapped so I did it up again.

I thought I'd better not go back on to the balcony again just yet. I lay on the floor in my bedroom and did a hundred sit-ups: the only exercise I could think of that didn't involve too much foot-work.

I felt good.

I felt drained and refreshed. Like a lanced boil. The world was my oyster. I rang up my agent.

Three days can be either a very long or a very short time. He didn't ask where I'd been, what I'd been doing, why I hadn't called. I usually called every day. Every other day at the outside. He had nothing for me. I still felt good. I didn't give a damn. I was going to be the new James Dean, and maybe I needed a new agent.

I drank about a gallon of coffee and made myself some more bacon and eggs. I felt tired after that so I lay down on my bed for a while with the curtains pulled. I slept for an hour and woke feeling even better. Light and full of energy.

I tidied my flat. I hoovered, dusted and washed up. I threw away all the old newspapers and went through my records and books, sorting out the ones I didn't want any more. I did the same with my clothes, and soon I had two black bin bags full of rejects.

I like to throw things out. The books and records I take to the library and the clothes I give to Oxfam. It makes you feel new, throwing things away.

I still felt energetic when I'd finished, so I stacked the records, books and bags of clothes on the landing outside my door, and went for a hobble in the park.

Half-way down the stairs I heard the phone again, but I didn't go back to answer it. It can take me hours, sometimes, to get out of my flat. I have a sort of ritual that will get me out when it's difficult. I turn off the oven at the wall switch. I unplug the television. I check that the immersion heater is off. I shut all the windows. The only trouble is that, as with all rituals, it's difficult to remember whereabouts in it you are at any given time and, of course, whether it's all been done. You've done it automatically, and the only way to be sure you've done it properly is to do it again, thinking about it this time. I get, for example, half-way down the stairs and I can't remember checking the immersion heater. I'm sure I did check it. It's part of the ritual to check it. It's just that I can't remember actually checking it. So I have to go back. I get out into the street and the same thing happens with the oven. I've been known to get half-way to wherever I'm going and have to turn back to make sure I've unplugged the television. I didn't want to get into all that today. I let the phone ring.

The park was like an oven. People were staked out on benches and on the grass, inert in the heat.

I found that by turning my foot sideways and rolling on the heel I could make good if ungainly progress. The section of the park up by Lord Holland's statue was deserted, which was odd because it was deliciously cool. I took my shirt off and went round to look at the peacocks, to see if maybe I could spot the one that had shrieked when I was on my balcony.

They were too far back from the railings for me to see them clearly, though a couple of peahens did come over to see if I had any food. The birds were hot too: ducks with their heads under their wings, an enormous sweltering turkey, bantams, crowned cranes, two emus, and a baby ostrich. All sitting still under the sun. Even the greedy peahens were only half-heartedly soliciting.

The back lawn, by contrast, was loud with disco music and frisbee players. I went and sat on a bench overlooking the formal garden. I had only just sat down when I heard the cry of a peacock, and at the same time the bench pitched and tossed like a boat in a gale. I held on hard to the arm of the bench and stared out over the garden, trying to focus on nothing and regain my balance. The garden rippled.

I thought I was going to throw up, but I managed not to. I don't know how long the spell lasted, but everything looked more or less the same when I came out of it, so I guess not long. It must have been hunger. I hadn't eaten anything but bacon and eggs in three days, after all. I went to the café for a cup of tea and a salad. And maybe a chicken roll. And a Danish pastry to follow. Maybe two.

I loaded my tray at the counter and carried it through the café to the open-air bit at the back. I had selected my table and was about to sit down, when a sun-glassed woman in purple satin pants and a khaki shirt knotted under her breasts let out a shriek that put the peacock to shame.

Peter-Patrick! she yelled. Darling!

That's my name. Peter-Patrick. Peter-Patrick Moberley. Yes, I know. There isn't anything you can say about it that I haven't heard before.

Daisy! I screamed. I didn't know you were back.

She stood up and opened her arms. I put down my tray on the nearest table and flew to her bosom. Well, hopped.

I loved Daisy. I'd known her on and off for years. We had had, actually, a brief fling together when we were on the Seychelles working on my famous coffee commercials.

We hugged and kissed. She looked marvellous. Strappy gold sandals with purple-stained toe nails to match her pants. A tiny naked midriff, and golden hair knotted like a fountain on the top of her head.

She must have been at least *trente-douze* years old.

You bastard, she said. Why haven't you been answering your phone. I've been ringing all day.

I've been sick, I said. Let me get my tray, and I'll tell you about it.

Daisy – as I guess you've guessed, the knotted fountain of hair is a giveaway, it's more or less a trademark – is Daisy Seton. If you haven't guessed, well, go to the gossip columns. You'll find it all there. The best bits anyway. The worst bits make other headlines. Like a none too clean-cut divorce. Like a sizeable chunk of North Kensington drug abuse from which, in the early seventies, she made a happy and well-publicized comeback, before going off to spend a couple of years with a certain aged Spanish painter who, like the Stagecoach, shall remain nameless.

If I say spend a couple of years with, I do so advisedly, because I'm sure that that is all it was, although, with me at least, Daisy herself has never been anything but resolutely ambiguous on the subject. But I do have a fairly clear idea of what her sexual and emotional type is, and it isn't octogenarian surrealists. And it isn't me either, though on the Seychelles I thought and hoped that it was. I couldn't believe my luck when we made it.

He painted – the aged Spaniard, that is – a series of pictures of her, a reproduction of one of which is hanging on my bedroom wall. Rather a tacky compilation, I think, with more than a hint of photomontage about it. Boats, horse skulls, and Daisy clothed in white samite contemplating voluptuously what looks like an upturned Nazi helmet with a spider plant growing out of it. The old man's symbological powers I assume to be on the wane.

But he captured Daisy. The face is marvellous. Compassion incarnate. Because, underneath all the scenes that the paparazzi love, the drunkenness, the shouting, the silly public gestures like taking off her clothes in Regine's, and a whole hideous row of predictably disastrous liaisons with manipulative layabouts half her age, that's what Daisy is. Compassionate. She'd give her last penny to a beggar. She'd sit up all night to hold your hand on the day her lover left her. And always the right sort of compassion too. No wallowing.

Like today. After I'd fetched my tray and told her about the joblessness, the loneliness, the quasi-rape et cetera, all she did was listen and smile that glorious Daisy smile that looks so stunning on the front of *Vogue*, or on a travel poster, or in the last tired works of a former semi-genius, and there I was, healed. Which is quite an achievement really because, as you've begun to guess by now I'm sure, I do tend to wallow just a little.

The only difficult thing about Daisy is her son. I don't know who his father is, and I'm none too sure that she does. It might be any one of the actors, singers, playboys, grandees and spirit-sodden jerks who litter her generous past. I don't suppose he knows who his father is either and I don't suppose he cares, because boy does he know who his mother is! He has one of those dreadful dandelion names that people gave their children in the mid-sixties, Jonquil or Torquil or something. And he tyrannizes over Daisy like Tamburlaine.

Well, there you are, I've done it again. No compassion in me, you see. Because he is lame. Like Tamburlaine he has a club foot. Which doesn't excuse him for being a poisonous little toad, but should make one think twice, I guess, about bitchy remarks.

OK, Jonquil/Torquil, I'm sorry. Like Genghis Khan. He tyrannizes over Daisy like Genghis Khan.

He was with us on the Seychelles, so I know. We couldn't go anywhere without him. He even wheedled his way into one of the commercials. He's the little raven-haired darling fishing off the jetty in the water-skiing number. Daisy smiled at the producer and he fell like a ripe apple. The child got paid for it too.

Are you getting the message? I don't like that boy.

On the Seychelles he really got up my nose. No scenes, nothing like that, or only one anyway, but he was just always there. Daisy and I had to scheme for every moment alone together. And he wouldn't go to bed. Up till midnight every goddamn night, and we started shooting again at seven.

Daisy used to sneak out of her hotel room into mine after he was finally asleep. We were shattered. We certainly made Make-up work for its living.

A week before we left he succeeded in breaking us up. It was two in the morning. Daisy and I had just concluded a successful consummation under the mosquito net and were sweating contentedly over each other, when the telephone rang and I answered it to hear a plaintive Jonquil/Torquil voice say, Peter-Patrick, I'm scared. Is Daisy there?

No, I said. Why? Should she be?

I can't find her, he said. I'm scared. This man is bothering me.

Man? I said. What man? What do you mean, bothering you?

There's this man, he said. He wants to do things to me.

For God's sake, I said. What man. Your door's locked.

He wants to do things to me, he said.

So where is he now? I said. At the end of the bed? Watching you phone?

He's on the balcony, he said. He hasn't got any clothes on.

Let me get this straight, I said. There's a naked man on your balcony. And he wants to do things to you.

Daisy, all this time, was grabbing at the phone and I was fighting her off. I was not pleased. I was bloody furious. I slipped off the bed and Daisy landed on top of me on the floor.

Hang on, I said into the phone. I'll just see if I can find Daisy. Hang on.

I covered the mouthpiece and held the phone at arm's length with one hand, and held Daisy by the fountain-gold hair with the other.

If, I said, you let that little prick talk you into going down, you and I are through. I mean it, Daisy. I've had enough.

OK, she said. It's a deal.

I gave her the phone. All she did was hang up, and get dressed. I picked myself up from the floor and lay on the bed, watching her.

When she'd finished dressing she came to the bed and tried to kiss me, but I turned my head away. She left then, without saying a word, and after she'd gone, I tore the phone from the wall and hurled it at the door. The hotel replaced the phone without saying anything, but when we came to leave there it was itemized on my bill. One replacement telephone. The company queried the bill, and I ended up having to pay.

He left us alone after that. I guess Daisy told him that it was only for one more week and he could afford to wait. Daisy and I had a good time from then on. The shooting was over and we spent hours together. There was a tacit agreement that all we had was the week. It wasn't her fault that I wanted more.

I loved Daisy.

After that I came back to London and unemployment, and Daisy and Jonquil/Torquil left for Spain and the Great Man. All I'd had from her since was a brief chatter letter from New York, where she was en route for Florida and a new super whizzbang healer for Wonderboy.

I did not like that boy.

If you knew Daisy, you'd be greedy and jealous too.

Anyway, there we were, Daisy and I, all passion spent, having a cup of tea in Holland Park. I was basking in her smile and stuffing my face fit to bust.

You've lost weight, she said. How do you manage it?

I haven't eaten properly in days, I said.

You look good, she said. I love the hair. It's sticking up at the back.

I smoothed it down.

How is he? I said.

I had to say it.

I left him in Florida, she said. They made me. They said it was best. He's ill. They think it's bad that I should be there.

Bad for whom? I said. For him or for you? Or for both?

Both, she said. It's not just the foot. It never was. You know that. He is ill. They say he's punishing me. For the foot, I suppose.

We sipped our tea.

It does make sense, I said. It does make a sort of sense.

I looked at my foot.

How would you like another cripple to look after? I said.

I thought you'd never ask, she said.

I put her cup on my tray and took it back into the café. When I got back Daisy was standing by her chair.

Where are your bags? I said. Where are you staying?

At the Hilton, she said. I checked in for tonight.

You knew I'd ask then, I said.

It shouldn't take long to move you, I said. Will they make you pay for it if you don't stay tonight?

I've paid already, she said. It doesn't matter.

You'll have to put up with my cooking, I said. At least for tonight.

Shall we go? she said.

We passed the bird garden on our way out of the park. It was cooler now. The peacocks were roosting in the trees. A white peacock perched on the railing.

We walked by arm in arm, slowly because of my foot, and I thought, Who is to say who is supporting whom?

We went to the Hilton to collect her bags. There were a lot of them, so we took a taxi back to my flat.

We had dinner on the balcony. Not much. A scratch sort of pasta dish. Tagliatelle with olives and capers, one of my stand-bys. And afterwards we sat and listened to records, both of us putting off the moment when we'd go to bed.

When we finally went she cried for a while and then everything was all right.

All passion spent.

How wrong can you be?

My foot got better quickly over the next few days. Most of the swelling went down and the rainbow-hued bruise diffused. I took the strapping off without bothering to go back to the hospital. I had to be careful with shoes. About the flat, where I spent most of my time, I wore none at all. When I went out, all I could manage was sneakers, but as in the summer I rarely wear anything else that was no big deal. One evening we went to a concert and I tortured myself into my Gucci's, but I had to take them off half-way through.

We went out almost every night. We even went dancing and I evolved a graceful one-legged hustle. But I couldn't walk the next day, so we didn't go again.

My third and fourth toes took on a stolid stumpy look that they still retain. I guess I'm stuck with it. Un souvenir d'amour.

The days I still spent by myself because, of course, Daisy was working. I pottered around the flat. I even sunbathed on the balcony. It's amazing how you can cope with being alone when you know that in an ever-decreasing number of seconds it's going to stop.

I taught myself how to cook. I got quite good because Daisy's a picky eater. I spent hours shopping and devising interesting menus. *Cuisine nouvelle. Cuisine minceur.* All that. I would wake up in the middle of the night with recipes and meal plans racing through my head.

I'll be all right if I ever get a job advertising wholemeal pancakes. I toss very deftly.

My speciality was a towering melon water ice that was totally delicious and too healthy for words. I can wax quite lyrical on the subject of water ices. They have virtually no existence apart from their temperature. Which makes them almost perfect, if you think about it.

We were happy. Daisy didn't mention Jonquil/Torquil and I hoped she was at least getting used to the separation. She seemed to be. I wasn't complaining.

It was Daisy who decided we would throw a party for my birthday. I'm not all that keen on parties, but the intention was so obviously to give me pleasure that it would have been boorish not to go along with it.

Daisy knows about a thousand more people than I do, so I left the guest list up to her. I couldn't think of a single person I wanted to ask. I gave her my address book, and *carte blanche*. My only specification was that she shouldn't ask my agent, because if I was going to drop him, then now seemed as good a time as any.

I did the cooking. I prepared high-fibre salads and low-fat dressing. I cooked a massive Burgundian fish stew and a mountain of saffron rice. I made a bathful of melon water ice.

My foot was pretty well back in shape, but one foot was

much whiter than the other. I decided to go barefoot. If you've got it flaunt it.

I spent a gruelling session in front of my cupboards, during which I heartily wished back most of what I'd given the previous week to Oxfam. I decided on a GI-style string vest and khaki fatigues. These things take time. Whatever you think about faces, and I've never been able to make head or tail of them, there is an art can tell the mind's construction in the wardrobe. And a party is no time to fall down on self-presentation.

I was ready fully half a hour early, and sat around smoking and fussing and waiting to see what Daisy felt about things, as manifested by her clothes. When she did finally appear, to join me in a pre-celebration joint on the sofa, she was triumphant. She hadn't even nodded at fashion. A baggy white silk blouse and a full, full-length skirt in plum-coloured watered taffeta. And court shoes. I gave her a round of applause. Her hair was down over one eye like Veronica Lake. It took my breath away.

Like I said, I'm not fond of parties. Other people's are all right, because you can go after an hour. But you have to stay at your own.

The beginning wasn't so bad. I was kept busy making sure everybody was eating and drinking and circulating freely. But after that the dreadful moment came, the moment I usually choose to leave, when you look around and see groups of happily chattering people, none of which you can join. You stand there, not against the wall I hasten to add, but within striking distance of the door, trying to look animated and unalone. And someone always comes up to you. And you can never remember who they are.

Which is exactly what happened. An enormous grey whale of a man in a blazer and grey flannels floundered up to me.

Daisy said I'd find you here, he said. Happy birthday.

Thanks, I said. How are you?

Fine, he said. Daisy said we should have a chat. She's looking well.

Considering, I said.

Oh yes, of course, he said.

You have to make allowances, I said.

She'll get over it, he said.

Excuse me a minute, I said. I have to get a refill. How about you?

I'm all right, he said. Could you tell me? Who is that extraordinary girl. There. The one with the black eye.

I looked across the room. I saw what he meant.

She had obviously reached the position I was in before Grey-flannels came and spoke to me. The only difference was she wasn't pretending. She stood in a pool of quiet.

And she did look a bit odd. She was very tall, about six foot two, I should imagine, several inches taller than me anyway. She had short black hair and one of those wide-eyed, straight-nosed faces that betoken happiness, and a total innocence of all thought. She could make a fortune advertising dreamy holidays in faraway places.

And the clothes! You'd never seen anything like her clothes. A man's evening shirt with a straight black tie and waistcoat. A foamy white broderie anglaise flounced confection of a petti-coat, worn as a skirt. Bare legs and cowboy boots. Cowboy boots! Her black eye she had made no effort to conceal. In fact, presumably on the If You've Got It, Flaunt It principle, she was wearing a monocle on a thick black ribbon in the other eye.

That's Stella, I said. Or is it Bella? Beresford-Perceval, so I hope it's Stella. Come to think of it, it's Bella. Bella Beresford-Perceval.

Now why did I do that? I always do that and I've no idea why. I pretend not to know people's names. Like all that Jonquil/Torquil business. I know as well as anyone that his name is Jasper. I've known Bella Beresford-Perceval for years.

I know what you're thinking. You're thinking that no one on this earth is called Beresford-Perceval. You think I'm making this up. Well, you're right, up to a point. When I first knew Bella, before she was married, she was plain Bella Lynch. I'm sure no one in the world is called Beresford-Perceval, but Bella's husband wasn't to know that when he invented it.

She's quite something, Grey-flannels said.

Isn't she though? I said. She's married. And frankly, I'd be careful of the husband.

Oh well, he said. She's quite a girl though.

I'd better fill up, I said.

Now don't forget, he said. I want to talk to you. Daisy said she was sure we could work something out.

I headed for the balcony. I needed some air. There wasn't much on the balcony. But it was evening, and summer evenings I love. I could live in a cellar, if it weren't for summer evenings. They look cool. They cool you. Even if, like this one, they were positively hot.

The trees in the park were quite still. I leaned my elbows on the balustrade and watched my sweat drops fall into the garden. A voice, a low Irish voice, said, Hello, Peter-Patrick, and I turned round.

Hello, Bella, I said.

She was carrying one of my melon ices. I'd scooped the flesh out of the rind and filled it up again with the finished ice. She leaned on the balustrade next to me and laid her ice cold hand on my forehead. The scarlet varnish on her nails was chipped and blotched.

How's Jack, I said.

He's inside, she said. I haven't seen you for ages.

I guess I'll see him later, I said.

No, she said. Inside. GBH.

My God! I said. You mean? When?

Oh, ages ago, she said. You haven't seen us in years, you know. He'll be out soon.

How did you hurt your eye? I said.

I trod on a rake, she said. I really did.

GBH, I said. Well, well.

He got drunk, she said.

Got drunk, I said. That implies a sober state to start from.

22

He got into a fight, she said.

And that, I said, implies that he was ever out of them. A spell inside will give him a rest.

Oh, he'll be out soon, Bella said.

What are you doing? I said.

I'm waiting, she said.

You may not have guessed it, but Bella is a bit dim. Those lovely vacant eyes give you exactly what they promise – vacancy. She has to be the thickest person. I know. When you first see her, always in the background, always in someone else's shadow, all you can think is, There she is. Tranquil, placid, serene. Then you speak to her, and you realize, serene nóthing. This girl is dim. Just the sort of person who really would step on a rake.

I'd first met her about ten years before in Ireland. Actually, it was her mother I met first. Hal Lynch, sculptress and confirmed alcoholic. She drank herself to death a month before Bella married Jack. She was a crazy lady.

I met her – where else? – in a pub. You meet most people in Dublin in a pub. I was over there working in a play. You've got to start somewhere. I could fill pages with anecdotes about Hal, but I'll just give you a swift idea, because she's only relevant to let you know the context Bella was used to, the shadow Bella lived in.

In the pub she told me that she lived in a glass house, and I had visions of a sculptress-type, Frank Lloyd Wright dwelling in a fold of the Wicklow Mountains. She looked and sounded like a lady that might live in such a place. She invited me to tea there the next day and I arrived to discover that she meant what she said. She and Bella lived in a greenhouse at the bottom of someone's garden. It was a big greenhouse – it needed to be to accommodate the two of them, Hal's sculptorial accoutrements and several crates of Jameson Ten – but it was a greenhouse.

Tea, like breakfast, lunch and dinner, and most of the time in between with Hal, was whiskey. Bella made some toast I remember, and there was a cake. But mostly whiskey.

The last time I saw Hal was a few days before they finally took her away to St Patrick's to dry out, or die, or as it transpired both. It was at a ferociously toffee-nosed party in Ballsbridge. She caused rather a stir because she needed to pee and simply squatted on the lawn where she happened to be standing and did so. In the middle of a conversation with the director of the Irish National Gallery, where a significant number of her works still are.

Everybody said in the pub, after the shock of Hal's death was over, that now was Bella's chance. Chance for what, I'm not sure. Peace and quiet, maybe. But whatever the chance might have been for, Bella didn't take it. Or maybe in her own way she did, because, as I said, within a month she had married Jack and swapped Hal's shadow for Jack's. That was a case of out of the frying pan into the fire, if there ever was one.

When Jack was sober he was a concert pianist. You couldn't believe much of what he said. When he was drunk he was dangerous. I met him, in a pub of course, shortly after I arrived in Dublin, before I met Hal. He had either the most chequered past or the most forked tongue I had ever come across. He had been, he said, at various times, a diamond smuggler, a pupil of Cherkassky's and a disciple of the Krays. He used to call himself Lord Perceval until he climbed high enough to see that that wasn't fooling anyone.

He rarely paid for a drink. His usual practice was to go on a tour of pubs, drinking a barrelful in each, and when it came to payment time he'd offer the landlord insurance. The landlord, of course, would reply that he was fully covered and Jack would smile thinly and say, No, not that kind of insurance. It usually worked because Jack looked dangerous. And if it didn't work he swiftly became dangerous. He'd break a bottle or a glass against the bar.

Bella, through all this, would just stand there, waiting placidly until it was all over. More often than not she'd come back the next day and pay. How he stayed out of serious trouble I'll never know. Maybe Bella's purse had something to do with it. Hal's death had left her fairly well off. Or maybe he was every bit as dangerous as he said.

I lost touch with them after I left Ireland. Then some five years ago I bumped into them in Antiquarius, where Bella had a short-lived stall selling lace, and saw them occasionally afterwards. They hadn't changed. I was tired of all that rackety stuff.

I went to a couple of parties in their house in Putney, where Jack and his cronies drank and shouted, and Bella vainly and vaguely tried to keep things *soigné* with candles and tablecloths and long dresses. I soon gave up going. I imagine Daisy found their names in my address book and asked them. It's a depressing business keeping an address book up to date.

So what did he do? I said.

He hit someone, she said. The wrong person this time. With a broken glass. It's not that serious. He only got two years.

Two years, I said, seems serious enough to me.

Not for GBH, she said. You get quite a bit for that.

I can't see him getting time off for good behaviour, I said.

Well, a bit, she said.

She put her ice-cool hand on my forehead again.

Better? she said.

We'd better go back in, I said. It's my party.

I'll stay here for a while, she said. Eat my ice.

It's melted, I said. Look.

I took the melon rind from her and poured the melted ice over the balustrade.

I'll get you another one, I said.

No need, she said.

Well, I said.

You don't have to run away, she said. We could both stay out here together. We don't have to talk.

She jumped up and sat on the balustrade. I nearly jumped out of my skin. We were forty feet up.

Christ! I said. Don't do that.

She smiled. I can't stand that. I felt sick.

Bella, I said. You're making me feel sick. Get down.

She carried on smiling. She put both palms on the parapet and leaned back.

Bella, I said. For fuck's sake.

She clasped her hands round her left knee and leaned further back.

A peacock shrieked in the park. I fled back into the drawing room.

What on earth did the silly bitch think she was doing?

The party was in full swing. I couldn't see Daisy anywhere. I saw Grey-flannels heading in my direction but I escaped into the bedroom.

I was just in time to see Daisy put down the phone. Through the window I could see Bella still perched on the balustrade. Daisy was crying.

How is he? I said.

I didn't get through, she said. I tried, but I lost my nerve.

Shall we go? I said. We could go for a walk in the park. See the birds. Let them get on with it.

Did you see O'Brien? she said. O'Brien and Caine. I told him about you.

I don't know, I said. What does he look like?

Peter-Patrick, she said. I fixed it up. He wants you.

I don't know, I said. I don't know what he looks like.

Grey, she said. He looks like a grey whale.

Oh God, I said. I've seen him. Why didn't you let me know? I'd better go find him.

Daisy looked at the phone.

Go ahead, I said. What harm can it do?

Peter-Patrick, she said. Go and talk to O'Brien for a while.

I looked out of the window. Bella had gone.

Silly bitch, I said. I hope she didn't fall off. God knows she's thick enough.

Peter-Patrick, Daisy said. Go away for a while. Please.

I found Grey-flannels at the drawing-room door.

How's Daisy? he said. I thought she looked a bit peaky.

She misses Jasper, I said. She'll be all right.

Yes, Grey-flannels said. She told you about me?

Oh, yes, I said.

Well, he said. Do you think we'll get on?

What a question, I said. I'm going to turn down O'Brien and Caine?

That's all right then, he said. Come and see me tomorrow. Well, I'll just go and say goodbye to Daisy.

I leaned against the doorpost. O'Brien and Caine make my poor agent look like a hick hack.

I headed for the drinks trolley again thinking, Daisy is my darling, my darling. I fixed myself a large vodka and Daisy came in.

OK? I said.

Sure, she said. Why not?

I hugged her.

I love you, I said.

Let's dance, she said.

I wonder what happened to Bella, I said. Maybe she did fall off the balcony.

We danced.

I enjoyed the party on the whole. I thought that between us we had some nice friends.

At one o'clock it didn't matter how nice they were. I wanted them to go. Daisy and I turned our backs on the last determined merry-makers, locked the bedroom door and went to bed.

Daisy was feeling amorous but all I wanted to do was sleep. Whenever I shut my eyes I saw Bella's face.

Later, when Daisy was asleep and the last junketers had departed, I got up and went to sit for a while in the drawing room. It already had that deadly post-party smell. Stale food, stale smoke, stale everything.

I felt light-headed and hollow. Over-stimulated and over-tired. I fought my way over a mountain of debris into the kitchen and made myself a cup of hot milk, which I took out on to the balcony and sipped looking over the park.

I leaned on the balustrade, neither awake nor asleep. I kept on seeing Bella out of the corner of my eye, standing in the doorway or sitting next to me on the balustrade. Once I nodded right off.

I jumped awake and knocked my milk down into the garden, the cry of a peacock echoing in my ears.

I went back to bed at four o'clock with the sky light and the birds singing in the morning.

I woke up at seven to find myself in bed with Bella. I shook my head and it was Daisy again. I kissed her. She curled up tightly against me and I went back to sleep.

All the next day – Daisy got up early to work and I spent the morning and part of the afternoon tidying the flat – I couldn't get Bella, or the image of Bella, out of my mind. My eyes were particularly bad and I had to put drops in them more or less every hour.

I telephoned Grey-Flannels at lunch-time and made an appointment for four. Throughout the interview, which was more of a chat really, in his surprisingly shabby office in Hay Hill, I saw Bella's face every time I blinked.

The upshot of the chat was that he agreed to take me on provided that I could tactfully drop my present agent. I foresaw no difficulty in that area. I imagined he'd be fairly glad to get me off his hands. I called him when I got home. He wasn't surprised. I told him I was opting out for a while. Maybe I'd go to the States with Daisy.

I rang off and called Bella, but she wasn't in or didn't answer.

Daisy got back tired and low so I took her to the movies – *Casablanca* and *The Maltese Falcon* at the Electric Cinema. Old favourites – and we went to bed early.

I woke up thinking of Bella. Planning to call her and meet for lunch. It was, I felt, about time I saw her and treated myself to a dose of reality. It was pissing me off seeing her face everywhere and I thought a sight of the real thing would break the spell.

I was wrong. It was like the awful moment when you realize

that the person sitting next to you on the train is going the whole way and you're just going to have to sit it out. I was going to be stuck with Bella for some time.

I knew, even as I was saying it, that it was a mistake to tell Daisy that I was going to spend the morning shopping in the King's Road and maybe drop into the Markham for lunch.

For a start it meant that I'd at least have to go to the King's Road and buy something. Secondly, I had never before told Daisy how I was going to spend my day. Nor had she asked, and my volunteering the information could only let her know I wasn't being strictly truthful. Thirdly, she wouldn't have given a damn if I'd come right out with it and said that I was going to spend the day with Bella. People see their friends every day. Sometimes sleep with them too, as I had every intention of doing with Bella. It's the best way of exorcizing an obsession that I know.

Daisy looked at me oddly and said if I was going out could I buy a new 100-watt light bulb for the hall. I looked at the floor and swore to myself. This business with Bella was obviously going to be difficult.

I spent as little time as possible in the King's Road. I had a good idea of what I was going to buy. It was going, I had decided, to be a preppy autumn. I bought a pair of black trousers and a blue and grey flecked tweed blouson with padded shoulders. At Antiquarius I bought a huge cotton art deco shawl for Daisy, then headed straight for Putney.

Bella lived in a – of course – ramshackle semi in Southfields. Combemartin – she pronounced it Combermartin – Road. When I first came to London way back in the sixties and was overwhelmed by the chic of it all, I used to walk up and down and round the block outside places like the Colville, screwing up my courage to walk nonchalantly in. And so I did in Combemartin Road. I walked past Bella's house with my eyes fixed straight ahead, rehearsing casual phrases of greeting, walked round the block and sat on a garden wall for a bit. I almost gave up and went home. There is no greater distance than that

29

between you and somewhere you can't quite bring yourself to be. The only way to cross it is to empty your mind, stop forcing it and worrying about it, and act. Which is what I did.

I jumped off the wall, marched down the road and up to Bella's door without a thought in my head and rang the bell. When she answered it she looked, as usual, awful. A rather dirty madras smock and yellow flip-flop sandals.

Hi, Bella, I said. Just passing.

I saw you, she said. Walking by. I wondered when you'd come.

Her teeth were stained, I saw, and her hair would be the better for a wash.

I was just doing the ironing, she said.

The house – of course – was an appalling mess.

Or what I saw of it. Two rusty bicycles dying in the hall. A smell of ancient cooking, damp and whiskey. Bella took me into the front room. Her ironing board was set up in the window by nicotine-yellow net curtains. Newspapers, coffee cups and unwashed plates littered the floor. In one corner was a rather good Steinway grand with the string frame extracted and leaning against the wall behind it.

I sat on a sofa that smelled of cat while Bella made coffee. I didn't dare follow her into the kitchen. She stuck her head round the door.

There's no milk, she said.

Par for the course, I said. I'll have it black. No sugar.

Will you have some whiskey in it? she said.

Why not, I said. It'll take away the taste.

When the coffee was ready Bella went back to her ironing. I tried not to look. Flimsy and holey items of intimate apparel draped the back of a chair. I crossed my legs to conceal, or accommodate, an erection. I couldn't think of anything to say. Bella ironed and supped coffee. Mine went cold.

Did you like the party? I said.

Oh yes, she said.

30

You got home all right? I said. I looked for you but you'd gone.

I enjoyed it, she said.

It went on a bit, I said. But it was OK.

Coffee all right? she said.

Fine, I said.

I wanted to scream. I wanted to grab her, and ravish her across the ironing board.

That's that, she said. Unplug it for me, will you?

I unplugged the iron and she sat next to me on the sofa. I still couldn't think of anything to say. I put some drops in my eyes.

More coffee? she said.

No thanks, I said. I've still got this.

She put her hand on my leg.

Poor Peter-Patrick, she said. I've got to go soon. It's visiting day.

I can't stop thinking about you, I said. I can't get you out of my head.

It wouldn't be fair, she said. To Jack. To Daisy. To you. Or to me.

I'd better go, I said.

Come and see me again, she said.

Give my regards to Jack, I said.

I thought my trousers would burst. Bella stood up and put her hand on the top of my head.

Poor Peter-Patrick, she said.

I remembered the light bulb on the way home. I got off the bus in High Street Kensington and bought one in Barkers. Then I walked home across the park.

I stopped at the bird section to look at the peacocks. They were all asleep in the sun except for the white one, which came up to the fence and pecked at my trouser leg.

Suddenly I didn't like myself at all. I clenched my hands on the railing and gritted my teeth. I ground my eyes shut and when I opened them there was a brown haze in front of my vision.

The feeling passed. The haze dissipated. I noticed that the white peacock was pecking at my clenched hand. I slapped its head hard and walked away.

Daisy was home when I arrived back at the flat, and the first thing she asked me was whether I'd got the light bulb. When I fitted it, it turned out to be the wrong wattage. Only sixty, and Daisy screamed at me. She raged and swore. She called me an idle bastard who sat on his ass all day while she worked. A selfish, ignorant fool who couldn't be relied on to do the smallest thing for her. Among other things. I was so surprised that I just stood there with my mouth open and she flung herself into the bathroom only to emerge again a few seconds later, white in the face and shaking.

You've left the fucking lavatory seat up, she said. Don't you know any fucking better than to leave the fucking lavatory seat up when there's a fucking lady in the house.

She threw herself back into the bathroom, slamming the door, and I heard the sound of running bathwater and sobs. I went into the kitchen and started preparing supper. When I was draining the rice Daisy stuck her head round the door.

Some lady, she said.

Had a hard day, dear? I said.

I'm sorry, she said.

Get out of my kitchen, I said. Go into the drawing room and look in my bag.

She went, and came back wearing the shawl.

It's beautiful, she said.

So are you, I said.

Together we finished making supper. While we ate, I was making plans for the next day: the gym in the morning, now that my foot was usable again, and a visit to Bella in the afternoon.

We drank a lot of wine at supper and afterwards we lay on the sofa and watched television. At least, I watched. Daisy curled up with her head in my lap and went to sleep. I stroked her hair, thought of Bella, and felt like a heel. At the end of the programme I woke her up and we went to bed. This time it was Daisy who was sleepy and me who felt amorous. I had a difficult day to get rid of. I didn't feel any less of a heel when I'd finished.

Next morning, after Daisy had left. I had a mammoth session in front of the mirror. I inspected myself from crown to instep. Always a soothing process, even if the results of the inspection are not uniformly encouraging.

It was a fortnight since I had broken my foot and the only exercise, if you could call it that, I'd had in that time was walking and a hundred sit-ups a day. Not enough. I was swelling visibly. I was still dark brown except for the broken foot. My hair and beard had grown. I didn't look a bit like James Dean. There were bags under my eyes. The skin on my face looked waxy and porous. I was clearly overdue for a facial, a trip to the hairdresser and one hell of a work-out. Which was OK because the next most soothing thing to a session in front of the mirror is one hell of a work-out. It concentrates the mind wonderfully.

I telephoned Bella and asked if she wanted to come over for lunch. She couldn't come so I said I'd drop over and see her about three o'clock and headed for the gym. I worked out for two hours, had a sauna and a massage, and everyone clucked over my foot and told me how sexy my beard was.

Afterwards I felt more relaxed than I had for weeks. A lot had happened in the last fortnight. Notably, I was on the books of about the best agency in town and I was in love with two women. Not that much had come of either of these two developments as yet. In fact the two-women part was showing signs of being a mixed blessing. But after a massage, and with the prospect of a haircut and a facial, the world takes on a rosier hue.

Unfortunately the rosy hue didn't last longer than a couple of hours and I needed it for longer than that. The next week was difficult.

I saw Bella every day. Every morning after Daisy left I called her and asked her if she'd come over. For lunch. For a walk in the park to look at the birds. She wouldn't ever come. I'd spend the morning in the gym and go over to her house in the afternoon.

Those visits were not fun. I never knew how I felt. As I said, Bella was so stupid. Most of the time we simply sat there without saying a word. And yet when I wasn't there I could think of virtually nothing but when I was going to see her again.

I dragged myself away every day at half past four and as soon as I had closed the door behind me I would be planning the next day. How I'd buy her some flowers, maybe a bottle of wine. Maybe I'd even be able to get her over to my place. I knew I'd never be able to have my way with her in her own house. But in mine. Home territory and all that. Possibly she wasn't quite as stupid as I thought, because, as I said, she never came.

TWO

I didn't set out to be a model. It was never meant to be anything but a second string. I set out – God help the poor bastard, who doesn't? – to be an actor. I passed out of Webber Douglas in a blaze of something like glory, and set off to conquer the world. I began – don't ask me why, it's another story – in Ireland, and achieved pretty considerable success (the lead part in *Hair*, that sort of thing) on the strength of which I came back to London, where I sank like a stone: walk-ons in sit-coms, small fringe groups, the faithful old retainer with a line and a half in *Sense and Sensibility*, an episode or two of *Z Cars* if I was really lucky, and the ultimate pinnacle of chorus work in a West End production of *The Pyjama Game*.

I hated it. I got close to despair. I thought of jacking it all in and retraining as a postman. Then one day I was sitting leafing through my old press cuttings and it struck me that some, if not all of the photographs made me look spectacularly glamorous. And here I'd better say that although I am not exactly one to crack a mirror at fifty yards, spectacularly glamorous I am not. That is one of the many meretricious things about my chosen profession. It isn't based in any way on how you look. It's based on how you photograph. You can be the most beautiful man on legs. You can cause heads to spin, knickers to cream and hearts to break, and that's no guarantee that you're going to make it. The camera is an accomplished liar and you could end up looking like a wellington boot. Similarly, you can be just sort of OK, and the camera can make you look like the archangel Gabriel.

It doesn't make life any easier. I mean, you worry. Why, you think, is it not like the magazines? Why does everyone I ever come across look like the boy next door on a bad day, and there are the magazines just packed to bursting with people to turn your knees to water and your stomach to glass? Still, you say to yourself, at least they're out there somewhere. I may never see them except maybe fleetingly out of the corner of my eye as I wait for a bus, and they've gone by the time I look again. I may scour the clubs and bars. I may spend hours standing around, or dancing by myself, and see no one whose looks I prefer to my own company. But they are out there somewhere. They have to be. They're in the magazines. And if they're there, then sure as hell I'll run into one some day.

And then, by some chance, you become part of that world yourself and you realize. Not only is life not like the magazines, but magazine people aren't like the magazines either. They are fat. They are flabby. They have bad skin. Their jaws jut, their teeth are crooked. Their eyes are off balance and their mouths are too thick or too thin. They have trouble shaving and they look, in short, just ordinary. Just like you.

It's a bitter moment. The fairy-tale world of beauty you've always relied on doesn't exist independent of the glossy page that displays it. It takes a good long time to realize that that, of course, is the secret of its beauty. Like what I said about water ices. These images have no existence apart from their texture. Which makes them very nearly perfect: as utterly divorced from reality as reality is divorced from perfection.

Anyway, after the blinding realization that I was photogenic, I became a model. And things looked up right away. I was in work. Most of the time. And the right sort of work too. None of those great trailblazing advertisements that rocket you straight up into the heavens and kill you stone dead for ever after. You have to be a Daisy to survive that, and even she had to work her butt off to survive that initial stardom. I got steady, minor work and I was rarely out of it. I didn't look back. You don't get too famous that way. But you do get comfortably off.

And also, of course, you get paralysed. There are no more walk-ons in sit-coms, no more episodes of *Z Cars*. But these, hell though they are, are the building bricks of the trade, and who am I to talk about the high artistic fulfilment of coffee advertisements anyway? You get secure in your second world and lost in your first one. In the end people get fed up with offering you acting auditions, no matter how seedy, when you're too busy with your modelling work to go to them, and you daren't give up on the modelling because you've got too used to what it can buy. Then, as I told you at the beginning of all this, a time comes when you don't get any modelling calls, and then where are you? Out on a limb is where you are. Up shit creek is where you are. On your uppers is where you are. And not everyone can get you in with O'Brien and Caine, and give you a shot at getting back again.

There are, now I'm on the subject, other troubles too. Mainly in the self-image area. No matter how hard you try to remain a human being, with not too big a head, the fact remains that you do begin to consider yourself beautiful and therefore something wonderful and strange. The fact remains that you are your own commodity. You do become convinced that the way you look is most, if not all, of what matters, and that it matters as much to others as it does to you, and that details of your self-presentation cannot fail to be fascinating. If you're not careful – and I'm not careful – you find yourself passing on, as gold nuggets of news, the brand of shampoo you use, and the various secrets of how you maintain yourself. Like work-outs and facial saunas, and how many hours a day you spend on the rowing machine, or what time it's best to go to bed at night.

If your main concern is the way you look, the way you move runs a close second. Movement is a bitch. When you've been in modelling for a certain time your every gesture is studied. I don't want to spend too long on this. I want to get on with the story, and the subject's a painful one anyway. So I'll just mention the worst, the most insidious, thing about the whole business of movement. It makes for lousy sex. It makes you lousy in bed. I mean, not only can you not prevent yourself from thinking, I am a model, anyone on whom I decide to confer the benison of my body had better just think himself or herself lucky. But also when you do finally manage to get as far as the bed, your movements are so bloody self-conscious that you end up either pulling out all the stops and giving a virtuoso display of erotic performance, or going as still as a mattress. Neither of which makes for much fun. On either side.

And that's not all. The worst is yet to come. You judge people by the effect you have on them. You look into their eyes and see your reflection there, your snapshot in their pupil. And if they don't like what they see they don't exist. When I met Daisy at Heathrow on the way to the Seychelles, we kissed, took a step backwards, and inspected our images in each other's dark glasses. Our hands flew to our hair. I adjusted the knot of my tie. She twitched her blouse. OK, we both liked what we saw. OK, we both caught ourselves doing it and laughed. But the fact remains.

Daisy must have guessed that something was up. She would have had to be blind not to. She started giving me whole lists of little commissions, like the light bulb, to do while she was out. I never did them.

After my morning at the gym. I went and sat in the park and waited until it was time to go and see Bella. I lay on a towel and sunbathed. When it got too hot I went and watched the birds. I bought bags of grain at Holland and Barrett and fed the peacocks. After a while it got so that they recognized me and would strut over to the fence when they saw me coming. The white one ate from my hand. I must have fed it pounds of Original Crunchy with Honey and Raisin.

At three o'clock I'd go and spend an hour with Bella. And at five I'd be back at home cooking dinner for Daisy. The quality of the food alone must have told her that something was up, let alone the fact that I hadn't done a thing she'd asked me to do. She made no comment.

Except once. You can't spend hours in the park and in the kitchen, and I was skimping on the kitchen. Where I used to take pains, pounding things with a mortar and pestle, sieving,

40

peeling tomatoes, soaking dried ceps, I now bought tins, liqui-dized everything together, and hoped. One day, fresh back from Bella's, I chucked the ingredients for gazpacho into the Moulinex, whizzed, and chilled the result in the fridge. Daisy tasted it, put her spoon down, smiled and said, Hm, a type of gazpacho. And I knew the time had come to do something.

We were both, subject to the proviso I mentioned earlier, fairly vigorous in bed. Daisy, I guessed, because she loved me. I, I knew, because I loved her, and felt a shit about Bella. It was a bit joyless, all in all. After it was over we'd kiss, and turn our backs on each other and pretend to sleep. It wasn't my fault. I couldn't get Bella out of my mind. When I knew Daisy was asleep I'd get up and go on to the balcony. Once I fell asleep out there and woke up wrapped in a blanket. Daisy never said anything. She simply went to work every day, while I went to see Bella.

And that's how things went on all the way through July. Daisy didn't mention Jasper or try to get in touch with him. Every now and again I'd try to get her to phone him but she wouldn't.

Then one day at the beginning of August Bella agreed to come round to my place. I had had a lousy night. I had drunk a lot of wine at dinner and had fallen into a torpor at about midnight. At half past one I woke with a racking headache and a parched throat.

The room had gone into what I call white shift. I don't know if you know it. It happens to me a lot and it usually presages sleeplessness. Everything appears as if through a haze of foggy whiteness. Daisy was asleep. I got up and drank a gallon of water but it didn't make me feel any better.

I was blazing hot. I tossed and turned in bed for hours and when I slept I dreamed that I was tossing and turning for hours more. I counted the hours till five o'clock and the next thing I knew it was bright day and Daisy had gone.

I lay there dozing for a while, and was just about to drag myself out of bed to have a shower and call Bella, when the phone rang. It was Bella asking herself over for lunch. I agreed, of course. I couldn't believe my luck. I'd been asking her to no avail for weeks. I'd almost given up hope of her coming.

I felt better at once. I leaped out of bed, and whistled while I shaved. I put a bottle of the lightest, driest white wine in the fridge. I raced through my exercises at the gym and was back by twelve thirty, trying to decide on my sexiest outfit. In the end I stayed with the jock look I'd worn to the gym. Crisp white tennis shorts and shirt, sneakers, socks and headband. Dashing. Irresistible. I had no intention of being resisted.

She was late, of course. No one but a fool would expect Bella not to be late. She had said she'd be round at two, and fully half an hour before then my nerves were in shreds and I was raiding the kitchen. Some people smoke when they're nervous. Some people drink. I do both, but mostly I eat. By two o'clock I'd eaten the fridge virtually bare. Tomato sandwiches, salami sandwiches, the remains of yesterday's cassoulet, cold, and half a tub of yoghurt.

By quarter past two I'd opened the very dry white and had smoked myself hoarse. I paced round the flat twitching at curtains. I sat on the sofa and leafed through magazines.

By half past I was just sitting, staring at the wall and cursing. Shit. Shit. Shit. Shit. I went down to the front door and scanned the street. I left the door open and went upstairs again, still swearing. I put another bottle of very dry white in the fridge and finished the first one. I went and stood by the door. After what felt like a month the bell rang. I counted slowly up to thirty before I smiled and opened the door – and there was Jack.

Well, he said. Aren't you going to ask me in?
    Um. Yes, I said. Um. Hi. Come in.
    Surprised? he said.
    Jack, I said. I haven't seen you in years.
    Not surprising really, he said. Considering.
    When did you . . . ? I said.

Day before yesterday, he said. Look, it's lovely here on the landing, but . . .

Of course, I said. Sorry. Come in.

I was scarlet in the face. I took him into the drawing room and sat him on the sofa.

I'll get you something to drink, I said, and went into the kitchen. Mainly to hide my face till it cooled down.

Will wine do? I said. White wine?

Lovely, Jack said.

I ran the cold tap and doused my face.

Make yourself at home, I said. I won't be long.

I took the bottle from the fridge and put it to my forehead. I got some glasses and a tray and took them through to the dining room. Jack was sitting in the middle of the sofa, his legs splayed, his arms along the back, smiling.

Here we are, I said.

Yes, aren't we, he said. You look well.

And you, I said.

I've been better, he said. How's the wine?

I tried not to let my hand shake as I poured.

Cheers, he said. Happy days.

Cheers, I said. Welcome back.

You look great, he said. I love the beard. Thinner too. And brown.

Thanks, I said.

I got a bit slack inside, he said.

He patted his stomach.

Not much sunbathing either, he said. You look great though. Bella's told me all about you. Thanks for looking after her.

I drank some wine.

I appreciate it, he said. She gets lonely. She needs taking out of herself.

I smiled.

More wine? I said.

Thanks, he said.

I leaned forward with the bottle and he leaned forward with

43

his glass. I was about to pour when he dropped the glass and grabbed my wrist.

Oh God. I thought. This is it. Here we go.

No more wine, Jack said. Not just yet. Not just now.

He stood up and pulled me up with him. He kicked his fallen glass out of the way.

Put the bottle down, he said. Carefully now.

I put the bottle down and he took my other wrist. Slowly he drew both my hands up to eye level.

Not that slack though, he said.

He dropped my hands, took hold of my face, and squeezed.

I really like the beard, he said. It really suits you. I approve.

He let my face go.

I definitely approve, he said. Relax. I'm not going to eat you. I want to look at you.

He took a step backwards.

Jack, I said.

I want to look at you, he said.

Jack, I said.

Take your clothes off, he said.

Jack, I said.

Off, he said.

I took off my shirt and shorts.

Wow, he said. A jockstrap. Very sexy.

I took off my jockstrap. He ran his hands over my chest.

Golden brown, he said. Maybe I will eat you after all.

He bent down and took my cock in his mouth.

Jack, I said.

He licked my stomach.

Relax, he said. Like I told you.

He stood up and put his arms round my neck. He twined his fingers into my hair and pulled.

I undid his shirt buttons.

You're getting the idea, he said.

His body was very white.

A bit of a sag round the waist, he said. I'll soon get rid of it. All I need is a bit of encouragement.

I closed my eyes and he hit me round the side of the head.

Look at me, he said.

I opened my eyes again.

In here, I said. Or in the bedroom?

Here, he said. I think. Don't you? On the floor. Don't you think?

I stood very still while he took his clothes off and stacked them neatly on the sofa. An old grey suit. Pre-prison wear, I supposed. He kissed me and I kissed him back. This, I thought, is Bella's husband.

It was strange the way his desire took him. I expected to get hit, if not beaten, and roundly fucked. I got hit all right. Not too hard, for Jack, but plenty hard enough. But I didn't get fucked. The climax of the proceedings came when he threw me on my back, sat on me, and jacked off while I fucked him. Then we had a quiet glass of wine and a cigarette, and I went and had a shower.

A few minutes later I had dressed and was straightening up the room. Jack was in the shower when Daisy came in.

Hi, she said. I finished early. How was your day?

How was my day? I thought. How was my bloody day. I hugged her and gave her a kiss.

Fine, I said. How was yours?

Fine, she said. We finished shooting early. I didn't wake you when I left.

She sat on the sofa next to the neat pile of Jack's clothes.

Jack Beresford-Perceval, I said. He's in the shower. You know. Bella's husband. She came to my party. Would you like some wine?

Jack came in from the bathroom, wrapped in one of Daisy's towels.

Well hello, he said. Peter-Patrick, what have you been keeping from me?

I introduced him to Daisy and went into the kitchen to fetch

45

some more wine. I tried hard to figure out how things could be worse, but I couldn't do it. I got a new glass for Daisy and went back into the drawing room. Daisy and Jack were sitting on the balcony. I found his glass and mine and went out to join them.

I got a bit slack inside, Jack was saying. But Peter-Patrick says he can get me back together. He's been showing me the best exercises. Hard work though.

He spends hours in the gym, Daisy said. You couldn't be in better hands.

I had trouble pulling the cork. Eventually, with a prolonged squelching slurp, it came.

Ah, Jack said. They're playing our tune.

In fact, Daisy said, you ought to join. I'm sure Peter-Patrick can fix it. Couldn't you, Peter-Patrick?

No need, I said. All you have to do is pay for membership. It isn't cheap, I'm afraid.

No problem, Jack said.

I mean, you could go with him, Daisy said. He could go with you, Jack. Help you out.

Encourage me, Jack said.

Sure, I said. Sure I could. Glad to. I go every day.

I've got nothing else to do, Jack said.

OK then, I said. Why not? We could start tomorrow.

Jack stood up.

OK then, he said. Tomorrow. What time shall I come round?

Oh, don't go, Daisy said. There's no need to go. Peter-Patrick, what's for dinner?

Nothing really, I said. Nothing yet. Meeting Jack has thrown me out. I could knock up something.

Or we could go out, Daisy said. Come out to dinner with us, Jack.

So Jack came out with us for dinner. We sat around the balcony first for a couple of hours and chatted. Or Jack and Daisy chatted. Mostly I just listened, and I had trouble doing that. They laughed and drank and chatted and drank and laughed.

46

Mostly I just drank. I joined in the laughter and said a few words every now and again for form's sake. I was thinking about Bella. What was she doing as we sat around laughing and drinking? Would I see her tomorrow? Or would Jack keep me too busy?

Then Jack went and put his clothes on and Daisy and I went to change. All the time we were changing she told me how nice Jack was.

Why are you being so quiet? she said. Don't you like him?

Sure, I said. Sure I like him.

He came to see you, she said. You're the first person he came to see. Fresh out of prison. You should talk to him.

I talked to him all afternoon, I said. Anyway, the way you go on, how could I get a word in?

Peter-Patrick, she said. You're jealous.

Jealous! I said.

Jealous, she said.

She laughed.

Jealous, jealous, jealous, she said.

I sat on the bed.

Jealous, I said.

I had to laugh. I really did. I lay back on the bed and howled.

Darling Daisy, I said when I could speak.

Darling, darling Daisy.

Dinner sparkled. We went to Leith's and had an uproarious time. Jack paid extravagant attention to Daisy and pressed his foot on mine under the table. Unfortunately he chose my injured foot. It was nearly better but I didn't want it trodden on. The first time he did it I pulled my foot away, but he found it again and trod harder, so I gave up. I was limping on the way home and Jack commented, so the whole story had to come out. I made it as funny as I could and emphasized my assailant's bitten tongue. We all laughed. Jack said goodbye at the door and kissed Daisy goodnight.

See you tomorrow, he said. I'll be round early, so we can have the whole morning.

Right, I said. OK. See you then.

Daisy was particularly affectionate that night. I guess she felt my jealousy needed assuaging.

Bang on ten the next morning there was Jack. To my surprise he insisted on joining me at the gym. Even more to my surprise he did all I did and more. He took out membership and paid cash. I dread to think where the money came from. He came back to the flat afterwards and we had sex on the drawing-room carpet.

And so every day thereafter. Every morning at the gym. Every afternoon on the carpet. And always the undertow of violence. The man frightened me. There was always a hand knotted in my hair, a foot in my face, my arm twisted behind my back, and it always went on just that bit too long. Once he bit my tongue. Always it ended in the same way, with him sitting on me and jerking off. I thought of Bella. Sometimes I thought of Daisy. Once or twice I even thought of Jack.

I saw more of Bella now I was fucking her husband. Daisy liked Jack. She used to ask him to come round in the evenings and he brought Bella with him.

At the best of times, it may come as a surprise to you to hear, I am not a sunny, funny person. I am not always, I admit it, fun to be with. I flatter myself that I'm not often unfun either. Just sort of neutral really. But I do tend to be quiet. When you're with someone every day there isn't that much to say. Let alone be witty about.

Jack was witty. Or at least he was around Daisy. He didn't say much to me. Daisy loved it. Evening after evening Jack would spend talking with Daisy, and I was left with Bella. I wasn't complaining, but nothing was being solved either.

We went out together. To clubs mostly, where we did the sort of thing people do in clubs, Jack and Daisy to the sound of gales of laughter. Bella and I just danced and drank. Sometimes, from the dance floor or from our table, I would look out at all the groups of people similar to our own, and wonder what on earth it was they found to talk about. Jack and Daisy talked nonsense mostly. But always, at the end of the night when we'd seen Jack and Bella into their taxi and were sitting in our own, Daisy would hum and chuckle and say how much she liked Jack, how much fun he was, what nice friends I had, what a sweet girl Bella was. I agreed. I wasn't going to be called jealous again.

The more I saw of Bella the more I wanted to see. I really craved her. Partly, I must admit, because I thought that if I ever did manage to have sex with her the infatuation would diminish and I would be able to see clearly again. But of course I never would get to sleep with her. Jack had seen to that. And by now I really did want to forget her.

The whole thing was getting out of hand. I was beginning to feel totally trapped. Jack had seen to that, too. As far as I could see there was no way I could stop seeing any of them unless I stopped seeing all of them, and I wasn't ready for that. I loved Daisy. I wanted to fuck Bella. I wasn't going to give up. And Jack, it appeared, was not going to give up on me. It all looked like a pretty good trap to me.

O'Brien and Caine struck me as a way out. I called Grey-flannels regularly. He was charming and friendly and encouraging. But no work came my way. It would have been something if I had some work even just during the day. It would have got Jack off my back at least. Or me off his. But nothing. Just hang in there, Peter-Patrick. We're waiting for the big one.

We waited.

We were, the four of us as usual, in Inigo Jones when I found out it was Daisy's birthday on September the third. I didn't know. She hadn't told me. We had all been to a play and had decided for once not to go on to a club afterwards, so we were sitting over a lengthy post-prandial booze. Bella and I were discussing the play. Or I was telling Bella what I thought of it. I hadn't enjoyed it much. Not that it had been a bad play, or badly done. In fact it had been rather good. But the lead part had been played by someone I had been at Webber Douglas with, whom I had always rather despised, and I was feeling sour. In the middle of one of my most persuasive critical flights, when mildly derogatory remarks were slipping from my tongue like oil and vinegar, Bella frowned and sighed and said, Peter-Patrick, I wish you'd stop. You haven't said anything nice all evening. Which rather took the wind out of my sails. When it became obvious that Bella, maybe because she couldn't think of anything nice to say either, but more probably because she simply couldn't think of anything to say, was going to remain locked in placid silence – sometimes she really bored me, you know – I turned and listened to Daisy and Jack.

They were talking about work. Jack was saying that you should never, if you wanted to make a go of what you did, have something to fall back on, because if you did you always fell back on it. I nearly asked him what he felt gave him the right to say things like that, in what way he felt he had made a go of things, having just got out of gaol and all, but in view of what Bella had just said, and in view of what Jack himself could well put me through the next day on the carpet to pay for my spleen, I held my tongue. It wasn't always nonsense with Jack and Daisy. Sometimes they were serious. In fact, much of what I have palmed off as my own observations in the first couple of pages of this section – about modelling – is not my own unaided work, but a digest of what they said that evening. It upset me. Less because it was so patently pertinent to my case than because I felt that if Daisy was going to talk to anyone about that sort of thing, it should have been to me.

In fact, Daisy said, I'm thinking of giving it all up. I'm getting old. I've had enough. There's no future in it.

That froze me to my seat.

Daisy, I said. What on earth are you talking about? You haven't stopped working all summer.

I'm getting old, she said. Quit while you're ahead.

You've been working every day, I said. All summer. Every day.

I shall soon be forty-five, she said. If I had something to fall back on, I'd fall back on it right now.

Don't be ridiculous, I said. Forty-five. When will you be forty-five?

Which is when she said it. The third of September. Less than a fortnight away.

Jack, of course, leaped straight in.

A party! he said. We must have a party. Bella, we'll have a party. At our place.

In fact, Daisy said, I've nearly made up my mind. I've always planned to do it. Forty-five seems as good an age as any.

What a lovely idea, Bella said. Of course. It will be great fun.

What? I said. It seems as good a time as any for what. You've almost made up your mind to do what?

To give it all up, she said.

The third of September, Jack said. What day is that?

To go back to school, Daisy said. To get some qualifications and get a steady job.

What's today? Bella said. The sixteenth? No, the seventeenth.

To go to law school, Daisy said. I've always wanted to do it.

You're crazy, I said. Have you any idea of how many years that would take?

That makes it a Saturday, Jack said. Perfect.

I was going to tell you, Daisy said. When I'd made up my mind. I'm still making it up.

I want to go home, I said. I want to go home right now.

Daisy turned to Jack.

Actually, she said. I'd rather not. I was planning on spending the evening alone. With Peter-Patrick. Do you mind?

Oh, come on, Jack said. You can do that any time.

Not on my birthday, she said.

OK then, Jack said. The day before. You can have an official birthday. A party at our place on the second. We'll ask everybody.

Lovely, Bella said. Oh, Daisy, let's.

Yes, Daisy said. Yes, OK. I'd like that.

I want to go home, I said.

Although, Daisy said, come to think of it, Thursday would be better.

Thursday then, Bella said. Thursday would be perfect.

All the way home in the taxi I tried to get Daisy to tell me more. But she wouldn't. All she would say was that she hadn't decided. She hadn't made up her mind. She'd tell me as soon as she had. But what about me, I kept on asking. Where do I fit into all this? I mean, here you are making all these plans and I don't know anything about it. And why law, for God's sake? She was much too old to begin on something like the law. She didn't need to do it anyway,

You're rich, I said. You're famous. You've got all this work. You're Daisy Seton, for God's sake. What do you need to change for?

But she just kept on saying that she hadn't made any plans. And need didn't come into it. Not the sort of need I meant.

So why? I said. Where will you go? What about me? What about us?

Peter-Patrick, she said. We'll cross that bridge when we come to it, shall we? I told you. Nothing's fixed. Now drop it. Please. I'm tired.

I stared out of the taxi window till we got home and went straight to bed when we arrived. Daisy spent her usual half hour in the bathroom and when she came into the bedroom I pretended to be asleep.

Peter-Patrick, she said.

I didn't reply. She at on the edge of the bed. I could feel her looking at me for a long time but I kept my eyes closed. She kissed me, turned off the light and went away.

When I woke up a couple of hours later she hadn't come back. I got up and went through into the drawing room. Daisy was sitting on the balcony.

Daisy, I said.

She said nothing. I went out on to the balcony and knelt by her chair.

Daisy, I said. I'm sorry. Come to bed.

She was asleep. I kissed her till she woke.

Daisy, I said. I'm sorry. I'm sorry, Daisy.

I took her hands and she stood up. Something fell from her lap to the floor. When I picked it up I saw it was a picture of Jonquil/Torquil in a heavy leather frame. I hadn't seen it before. I gave it to her and she held it to her chest.

Go back to bed, she said. I'll be in in a minute.

I kissed her.

Come on, I said.

I'm trying, she said. Every day I try not to think of him. I miss him all the time. Go back to bed, Peter-Patrick. I want to be by myself.

You know what the doctors say, I said. You mustn't see him. It's part of the treatment.

It's just his foot, Daisy said. Only his foot.

Daisy, you know it isn't, I said. He's got to grow up like the rest of us. Please come in. I don't like to think of you alone out here. I love you, Daisy.

All right, she said. All right. I'll be in in a minute.

I took the photograph from her.

Where do you keep this? I said. I'll put it away.

In my briefcase, she said. The big black one.

Before I put it away I looked at the photograph again. Jonquil/Torquil was smiling bravely at the camera. I knew that brave smile. It meant that he was going to fight like the devil for his own way. No holds barred. Little brat, I thought. If that's the way you want it.

I put the picture into Daisy's case and went to fetch her from the balcony.

So things went on till the end of August. Daisy didn't mention her plan, such as it was, again and nor did I. I saw Jack every day. I wanted not to but Daisy liked him and I'd decided that what was all right with Daisy was all right with me. So I couldn't have broken with him even if he'd let me.

I saw Bella every evening – and the same thing applied. I thought I would be happy not to have to see her again. I wanted to concentrate on Daisy. But now Jack and Bella were part of our daily routine, so I had to endure her. Her bovine silences. Her unforgettable face.

Together, it appeared, they made Daisy happy. We turned our backs on each other less often in bed. Anything that took Daisy's mind off Jonquil/Torquil was fine by me.

I was really proud of Daisy's birthday present. I'd never spent that much money on anyone for a start. I bought her an enormous portable radio/tape recorder, a sort of musical suitcase. I used to take it out of its hiding place and look at it when I was alone. I got together a whole bunch of tapes to go with it. Any time Daisy said she liked a song at any of the clubs we went to, I'd take a note of it and record it as soon as I could. I enjoyed all the secrecy. I swore Jack to deathly silence and he helped.

The day of Jack and Bella's party, Daisy stayed home. I called Jack and told him not to come round, I wouldn't be going to the gym today. Daisy and I were going shopping. We ransacked the shops. Daisy bought, eventually, after hours of delicious indecision, popping from shop to shop and back again, and driving the poor assistants half-demented, a bronze-coloured watered taffeta ballgown. Very off the shoulders and narrow at the waist. Very Scarlett O'Hara from the waist down. And I bought a pair of baggy grey leather trousers and a matching blouson, with quilting, pleating and buckles in unlikely places, and a bootlace tie. All very special. So special in fact that I had to borrow money from Daisy to pay for it. By now the coffee commercial money was on its last legs.

Then we had tea at Brown's which always rather depresses me, but Daisy liked it. I can't stand the waiters. They embarrass me. When the tea arrived there was no lemon and all Daisy did was look around in an inquiring way, and there was an unctuous voice at one's elbow, murmuring that Madam looks as if she requires something. I hate all that Jeeves stuff. I mentally halved his tip and started teasing Daisy about her present to cheer myself up.

You'll never guess what it is, I said. Never. Go on. Try.

An electric blanket, she said. A canteen of cutlery. A set of Bristol wine glasses.

No, I said.

A weekend in Brighton, she said.

No, I said.

A Clarice Cliff pot, she said. A pair of silver salad servers.

No, I said.

One of those huge portable tape-recorders, she said.

I sat very still.

Oh Peter-Patrick, she said. I've guessed it.

You looked, I said.

No I didn't, she said. I promise. I didn't.

Jack then, I said. He told you. The bastard.

Peter-Patrick, she said. It was a guess. I didn't know.

It's spoiled now, I said.

No it isn't, she said. Of course it isn't.

Yes it is, I said. I shall have to get something else now.

Don't be silly, she said. That would spoil everything. You could have lied. You should have lied. You shouldn't have let me know I'd guessed right.

I'll be back in a minute, I said.

If the waiters in Brown's are embarrassing, the lavatory attendant is worse. All I wanted to do was pee, wash my face and lean my head against the wall for a while. You wouldn't believe how cast down I was. I could hardly believe how cast down I was. I was really depressed. My joyful surprise gone. My happy secret stolen. It had kept me happy for a fortnight. I could have wept. If it hadn't been for the attendant I might have done. While I was peeing he hovered. While I washed my hands he hovered. As I was seeing to my hair he spoke.

Does sir require his coat brushed? he said.

He flicked at my shoulders with a clothes brush.

I don't have dandruff, do I? I said.

The weather is very pleasant, sir, he said. Don't you think. Although the summer will soon be over.

Well, thank you for pointing it out, I said.

Does sir require a little cologne? he said.

For fuck's sake, I said. So I smell as well as having dandruff.

If that will be all, sir, he said.

He held the door open for me and I went out. Jesus, I thought, what sort of man do you have to be to earn your bread in some subterranean cavern oiling up to people while they piss? I forced a smile on to my face as I rounded the corner into the tea room.

I must be a good actor, because in no time Daisy and I were gossiping and giggling like all come up. I acted so well I almost managed to cheer myself up, and decided that I'd go out early the next day and buy Daisy something else. A Clarice Cliff pot maybe, or an electric blanket. I cheered up so much that I left a reasonable tip for Jeeves.

While Daisy was in the bath, I took out the musical suitcase. It was still a good present but the magic had gone out of it. I wrapped it up, and the tapes, in happy birthday paper and put them back in the wardrobe.

We both got into our party clothes and opened a bottle of wine. It struck me that Jack and Bella's was the sort of house you should eat before you went to, so we had a snack. Some *consommé en gelée*, some olives, an omelette and an orange salad. We smoked a swift joint and took a taxi to Putney. I told Daisy about the lavatory attendant, but not that I'd been rude to him. Daisy said he sounded rather sweet.

I knew Jack and Bella's parties from the old days and as soon as we turned into Combemartin Road and heard the thunder of old Rolling Stones records fully fifty yards from the house I knew I was not going to be surprised. Before the night was through people were going to be sitting, if not lying, on the floor and someone, with any luck not me, would be vomiting in a corner. There is a certain poetry in something that exactly fulfils your expectations and I settled in to enjoy it.

Bella opened the door for us, wearing her usual bizarre interpretation of party attire: espadrilles, frilly floral bloomers, and a houndstooth tweed hacking jacket. She took us past the living room, from which issued the raucous sounds of Jack enjoying himself above the music, and into the kitchen, where, as I could have predicted, she was madly making extra food for all the people who had turned up because Jack had got pissed the night before and asked everyone from the pub or club or wherever he happened to be, and probably the taxi driver who had driven him home. The entire room seemed to be draped in lasagne, and if I'd been Bella I'd have been in tears. She didn't seem unduly worried, although she did accept Daisy's offer of help. Just the thing, I thought. Ask someone to a birthday party in their honour, and make them help with the cooking. On the plea of going to get a drink for Daisy, I left them to it.

The living room showed signs of having been prettied up. Shawls were spread over what couldn't be shoved behind the sofa or under the table. A sheet flung over the piano turned it into a bar. There were candles in odd places and a selection of ill-matched chairs, already filled to overflowing with strangers drinking vodka out of tea cups. I noted with mixed feelings – the poetry of fulfilled expectation is short-lived – that quite a few people were already sitting on the floor. Music was bouncing off the walls. Jack, wearing what I sincerely hope was pastiche sixties (black flared trousers, tight from the ribcage to the knee, and a huge-collared orange crepon shirt), was enthusiastically asprawl on the sofa, clearly pretty far gone in his cups. It was going to be a long evening. Jack would be mortally offended if anyone tried to leave before the small hours and he tended to hit people who mortally offended him. When he was in his present state even people who only mildly got on his nerves were none too safe. It wouldn't have been a broken foot with Jack. More like a broken glass in the face.

I headed for the piano.

I guess it will seem strange in someone who intends, or wants, or wants to intend to be an actor, but I've always found entrances and exits difficult. I don't mind being somewhere, or someone, and I don't mind being someone or somewhere else. But the change is difficult. Crowded rooms are particularly difficult, especially if Jack is between you and the drinks. Ideally

I like to slip into a room and then just appear at your shoulder, drink in hand. I prefer film work to theatre work, cuts to exits and entrances.

This evening I was hoping that I could make it to the piano and have a drink in my hand, if not in my stomach, before my opening line. But that didn't suit Jack at all. I'd barely opened the door before he let out a roar, jumped up from the sofa and ran to embrace me.

Here he is, he yelled. The guest of honour. Peter-Patrick, you sexy bastard. Give us a kiss.

It's Daisy, I said when he'd finished kissing me. It's not my birthday. She's in the kitchen.

Everybody. Everybody, Jack said. Listen everybody. Someone turn that fucking music down.

I never thought I'd be sorry to hear the last of 'Nineteenth Nervous Breakdown'. Not only did someone turn the music down, they took the record off.

Listen everyone, Jack said. This is Peter-Patrick. I want you all to meet Peter-Patrick. The sweetest fuck in town.

So how would you handle an introduction like that? Some people laughed. Others shifted their feet and stared into the middle distance. I bowed and smiled.

You do me too much honour, I said.

As I bowed, Jack slapped my buttocks.

All in leather too, he said. Hands off everyone. This one's mine.

I thanked God Daisy and Bella were in the kitchen.

Jack, I said, can I have a drink?

Sure baby, he said. Anything for baby. Help yourself.

And having ensured that nobody would address a voluntary word to me all evening, he went back to the sofa.

More music, he said.

I went to the piano and spent a very long time fixing myself a very long drink. By the time I was ready to turn round music was bouncing off the walls again. Usually I would have scanned the room for faces I knew, or I felt might want to know me.

Not tonight. I didn't even glance. I leaned against the piano and drank. I swirled the drink in my glass. With great concentration I fished a long dark hair out from under an ice cube. When I'd finished, I poured three more and took them back with me to the kitchen.

Daisy was spreading layers of lasagne and sauce into tins and Bella was stacking them criss-cross one on top of the other in the oven.

Sorry it took so long, I said. I got waylaid. It's pretty busy in there.

Jack, Bella said, invited half London at the last minute. I think I've cooked everything in the kitchen.

I cleared a space on the table for the drinks. Daisy patted a final piece of lasagne home.

There, she said.

Bella pushed the tray into the oven and closed the door. For all I know the food is still there. I certainly didn't see it again.

We all sat down. Bella put her feet on the table.

Drink, she said.

We sat quietly over our drinks. I looked at Daisy and she smiled. I looked at Bella and she smiled. There was no comparison. The door-bell rang.

Let Jack see to it, I said. He asked them after all. Bella, I bet you've got a bottle hidden away in here.

The bottle was whiskey. The door bell rang and rang as we drank it. The music and the hubbub of voices got louder and louder. It was comfortable in the kitchen. We just sat around the table and made desultory, companionable chat. I felt good. We were half-way down the bottle before it struck me that they were waiting for me to go.

I stood up.

Ah, I said. Well. I guess I'll go back next door for a bit. Have some fun.

I have a nightmare memory from my childhood that sums up pretty much how I feel about parties. There were these friends of my parents, Mr and Mrs Broke, and every year they gave a big party for their children's birthday – Mark and Jane, I remember. Twins. I used to go hunting with Jane later, but at that time, it seems to me now, I only met them once a year at their party, an elaborate affair with a formal tea, where we all sat in rows and ate jelly and overfrozen ice cream that tasted of sugared milk and left flaky shards of ice for a long time on the tongue. After tea there was a conjuror, a bran tub, and party games. Musical Chairs. Spin the Bottle. Musical Statues. That sort of thing. And a particular horror called Hunt the Thimble.

I expect you know Hunt the Thimble. It wasn't the game that was horrible, but every year the same thing happened. We all had to face the wall while with much noise and business, many false starts and feints, to the sound of giggle and shriek and no peeking now, Jane turn back to the wall this instant, Mr Broke hid the thimble, and then Mrs Broke gave the signal, rang a bell, clapped her hands, and we all hunted for it. The person who found it won a prize and the whole thing started over again.

I knew what would happen. It happened every year. Everything would go OK. I'd face the wall and hunt the thimble like the rest. Maybe even find it and receive my tube of Spangles or a pack of chocolate cigarettes. And then I'd find myself standing against the wall for a long time with the sounds of all sorts of things going on behind me but no signal to turn round. What should I do? Had I missed the signal? Was all the noise behind me people looking for the thimble, or just the fun while Mr Broke hid it? Should I turn round? What was I supposed to do?

I stood there, facing the wall, trying to look as if this was nothing special, I'm just standing here looking at the wall, sort of thing I do all the time, hoping that soon, soon Mrs Broke would give the signal and everything would be all right. In the end of course Mrs Broke would see me and say, Who is that still facing the wall? Do you think he didn't hear the signal? What's that boy doing still facing the wall? And I would turn round, shaking with fear and fury, wishing fervently that I was dead, that Mrs Broke was dead, that I was safe back home in my room.

But there was another ordeal to be passed before that could happen. Again, every year the same. My father would arrive to take me home and Mrs Broke would say, You should have heard what your son said. What a coy child he is. Coy! I knew she was going to say it. Every year I was determined, if it meant spending the whole party without uttering, to give her no opportunity to say it but I never succeeded. I always said something. Something like, I hope it's fun at the pony club camp this year, or, Can I sit next to my cousin Erica, please? and Mrs Broke would say to my father, You should have heard what your son said. He hoped we'd all enjoy the pony club camp. He asked to sit next to his cousin. That child. Did you ever hear anything so coy?

The house was full to bursting when I left the kitchen. People lined the hall, sat on the stairs. The noise was enormous. Party bray and Bo Diddley in mutual strife. I fought my way through to the sitting room and stood by the piano. I'd just finished doing my eyes – smoke makes them even drier than usual – when someone in a shaggy black suit, shaggy shoulder-length blond hair, orange fashion sandals and a Nietzsche moustache who was pouring the contents of every bottle he could find – and there were quite a few of them – into a punch bowl, turned to me and spoke.

Liven things up a bit, he said. Chop up some fruit, why don't you?

He gestured with a bottle of fizzy Italian red towards a pile of apples, oranges and bananas on the edge of the piano.

Chuck it all in, he said. Liven things up. Seen you before somewhere. Pass us that gin bottle over.

I wouldn't mind a drink, I said.

Chop up the bloody fruit then, he said. Get the job finished. Know I recognize you from somewhere. Use this.

He fumbled a Swiss army knife from his pocket.

Chop them all up, he said. Slop them all in.

He emptied two more miscellaneous bottles into the bowl. I chopped up apples and oranges and added them.

Can't think where, he said. Know I've seen you somewhere. Don't forget the bananas. Always bring bananas for a punch. Gives it a zing.

On the bus maybe, I said, dicing bananas.

He stopped in mid-pour. Cider bottle in one hand, white port in the other.

Bus? he said.

He looked at me under his eyebrows.

Bus!

When people seem familiar, I said. It's often because you see them on a bus. Or a tube. Commuting, you know. You see someone every day on the bus and they get to seem familiar. Or the tube.

Tube, he said.

I tipped the diced banana into the bowl.

Or the tube, I said.

Good Lord, he said. You're quite right. I never thought of that. I could use that.

He finished pouring the cider and the port into the bowl.

Good idea, he said. Bloody good idea. I'll use that.

He dunked a wine glass into the mixture, held the full glass up to the light, brushed his moustache in it and sipped.

Not bad though, he said. Not bad at all.

I dunked a glass and drank.

That'll get things going all right, I said.

Care for a dance? he said.

I refilled my glass.

OK, sure, I said. Why not?

Nice suit, he said. I like the suit. I know where I've seen you now.

I'm that coffee bloke on the telly, I said.

He put out his hand.

Pleased to meet you, he said. I heard about you from Jim.

He looked around the room.

Came with Jim, he said. Can't see him anywhere now though.

We shook hands.

We'll forget the dance if you don't mind, he said. Take a raincheck. I'd better find Jim.

Later, maybe, I said.

He took my chin in his hand, and turned my face from side to side. Some of my eye drops had run out on to my cheek and he wiped the trace away.

Too early to say yet, he said.

He stood on his toes to look down at me. He bent his knees to look up at me.

Too early to say, he said. But I'd say you were in with a chance. What do you think?

I think I need another drink, I said.

Good idea, he said. Can't stand this sort of bunfight myself. I'll tell Jim I saw you.

He shouldered away through the crowd.

You've got to hand it to Jack, I thought. He sure knows how to pick them.

I turned back to the punchbowl.

You couldn't begin to describe the taste of the punch. I drank a couple more glasses. Someone took off Bo Diddley and put on Chubby Checker, and people screamed and did the twist. I was beginning to enjoy myself.

I pushed out into the middle of the floor, and twisted by myself. If it was good enough for the Stagecoach it was good enough for here. From the floor I saw Daisy and Bella at the piano, exclaiming over the punchbowl and helping themselves, so clearly their little powwow in the kitchen was over, whatever it had been about. Someone grabbed me by the hips from behind and pulled me back into his arms.

Hi baby, Jack said in my ear.

The man with the Nietzsche moustache went up to Bella and Daisy at the piano. Daisy threw her arms round his neck. Jack breathed booze into my ear.

Baby's looking good tonight, he said.

Nietzsche picked up Daisy and spun her round. They laughed and shrieked and hugged. Jack nuzzled my neck.

Why doesn't baby take me upstairs and fuck me, he said.

Who's that? I said. That man with Daisy.

Jack rubbed his nose in my hair.

Baby smells lovely, he said.

Daisy and Bella and Nietzsche looked across at us. They smiled and fluttered their fingers.

Jack, I said. Who is that guy?

He put his hands in my pockets and kneaded my crotch.

Daisy and Bella and Nietzsche carried on smiling and waving. I smiled and waved back.

Jack, I said through my smile, will you leave me alone and tell me who that man is.

Jack bit my neck.

Who cares? he said through his teeth. Who the fuck cares? One of Daisy's big shots.

I smiled across at them. I gestured at Jack and shrugged my shoulders. Jack wrenched me round to face him.

Will you look the fuck at me, he said.

OK, I said. OK. I just wondered who he was, that's all.

You are cute, Jack said. Oh yes, you're cute all right. But my God are you dumb! Give me a kiss and I'll leave you alone.

I closed my eyes and opened my mouth for a kiss. He took my face in his hands.

Remember, he said. You're not going to get a better offer all night.

He kissed the tip of my nose, tilted my face back and kissed my chin.

See you later, baby, he said.

I looked over at the piano but they had all gone.

After that, I twisted by myself again through the remains of Chubby Checker and jived through a generous chunk of Jackie Wilson, but the Swinging Blue Jeans, who were put on after that, were too much for me and I bobbed and weaved my way back to the piano for some more punch.

There wasn't much left in the bowl by this time. I had to tip it well forward and fish around with my glass amongst gobbets of sodden fruit. In the middle of this complicated manoeuvre an over-excited hippy hippy shaker set up a chain reaction that threw my neighbour into my shoulder and made me slop the bowl over the piano and the contents of my glass over my trousers.

I swore. They were expensive trousers.

I'm sorry, said my neighbour, a tall girl in a beige suit, with waist-length hair. I am sorry. What a mess.

I kicked an orange slice off my foot and picked at my sludge-stained leg.

Shit, I said. They're new bloody trousers too.

I'm sorry, she said. The piano's a bit of a mess as well.

Just look at them, I said.

I've said I'm sorry, she said. I don't see what else I can say.

I detached a fold of soggy leather from my thigh.

Sorry isn't going to get my trousers clean, I said. Sorry isn't going to get my leg dry.

Oh very well then, she said. I'm not sorry.

And she threw the contents of her glass at my chest.

In for a penny, in for a pound, she said.

Luckily there were a few bottles that had escaped the punch bowl. I helped myself generously from one of these. I didn't notice what it was. I just drank down a tumblerful and decided to call it quits for the moment. I was going to spend a while in the bathroom.

By this time I was really quite drunk.

I met Bella at the sitting-room door. She was leaning against a doorjamb, smiling at no one in particular.

Nice time? she said.

Just fine, I said.

She fingered the star of punch on the front of my jacket.

Accident? she said.

More or less, I said. Bella, I've got to pee.

There comes a time when you've got to be by yourself.

Nothing is more important than being by yourself. You would kill to be by yourself.

OK, Bella said. Have a nice time.

Daisy and Jack were sitting on the stairs.

Oh no, Daisy said. Your suit. What happened?

Don't ask, I said. Just don't ask, that's all.

Your suit. Jack said. What happened?

I went on up the stairs.

Of course the bathroom was full. Of course someone was waiting outside. It had to be Nietzsche.

Ah, he said. The man from the bus.

Hi, I said.

Or is it the train? he said. Could be the train. How's it going?

It's going fine. I said. I'm drunk as a skunk on your filthy punch. I'm drenched in the stuff from head to toe. Everyone keeps asking me. I'm fine.

That's good, he said. That's what it's for.

From inside the bathroom came the heavenly sound of the flush, promising relief, promising solitude. The door opened, and Grey-flannels came out.

This is getting silly, I said.

Hello, Grey-flannels said. I hoped we'd bump into each other. I see you've met Pip.

We've met before somewhere, Nietzsche said. We think it might have been on a bus. Or a train.

I really have to pee, I said.

Won't be long, Nietzsche said.

I leaned against the wall and waited. Grey-flannels leaned against the wall next to me. He wasn't wearing grey flannels this evening. He was wearing crumpled linen. Yellow crumpled linen.

I'm glad you've met Pip, he said. He seems to like you. That's half the battle.

I couldn't think of anything to say.

I mean, I'll keep on working my end, he said. With any luck I'll have something for you soon.

I still couldn't think of anything to say. I felt a bit sick actually.

66

Pity about your suit, Grey-flannels said.

I'll wash it, I said. I expect it'll come out. I'll damp it down as soon as I get into the bathroom.

He likes you, he said. That's the main thing. There's still a way to go, of course. I'll keep working on it.

My stomach heaved. My mouth filled with bile. I swallowed.

I can't tell you how much I need a pee, I said.

Well then, Grey-flannels said, detaching himself from the wall. I'll just see if I can find Daisy. Tell her the good news. I take it you're agreeable in principle.

Nietzsche emerged from the bathroom.

You bet, I said. I'm agreeable as hell.

That's good, Grey-flannels said. Pip and I'll just go and tell Daisy then, shall we? See you.

See you on the bus, kid, Nietzsche said. Don't forget I owe you a dance.

I smiled.

They moved off. With much after-you-no-after-you they breasted the top of the stairs.

I dived into the bathroom.

Ordinarily, you can well imagine, Jack and Bella's bathroom would not be an ideal place of refuge. Fluff tumbled round the claws of an aged Edwardian bath/shower whose lime-clogged taps and nozzles showed how often it was used. A tumble of shaving- and make-up gear filled the sink. The floor was bare planks dappled with indeterminate liquid. For some reason the lavatory bowl was rimmed with strands of long dark hair, presumably Bella's. I hate to think what she had been doing.

I was determined not to be sick. I held my breath while I peed. I scooped the clutter out of the sink, washed my face, did my eyes and dampened my hair. There didn't seem much point in trying to clean my suit. It looked pretty irredeemably stained to me. But I dabbed it with cold water just in case.

My stomach turned upside down. I clutched the edge of the sink and gulped as hard as I could. I was sweating and felt very cold. I caught sight of myself in the mirror. I would have been white if I hadn't been so tanned. As it was I was a particularly vile shade of grey. What the hell? I thought, and threw up into the sink. Almost immediately I felt better. My face in the mirror turned from grey to beige. I washed the sink, rewashed my face and sat on the edge of the bath.

There was a laburnum tree outside the window and I looked at its blossoms drooping against the night air. I was still pretty drunk. Suddenly and inexplicably I had an erection. I toyed with the idea of jacking off, but the impulse passed and I went down to find Daisy instead. It was a long time, I felt, since I had told that I loved her.

It wasn't Jack and Daisy sitting on the stairs as I came down. It was Bella and Grey-flannels. I don't know why I was so surprised. As I rounded the top of the stairs I saw him slip an elephantine arm round her shoulder and her muscles tauten with revulsion. It made me grit my teeth too.

Excuse me, chaps, I said. Just passing through.

Grey-flannels untwined his arm from Bella and they stood up.

Seen Daisy? I said.

In the dining room, I think, Bella said.

She was, Grey-flannels said. That's where she was when I saw her. She was talking with Jack. You've got a lovely girl there, you know.

He blinked.

You should hang on to her, he said.

I intend to, I said.

He blinked again.

Look after her, he said. It's easy to hurt Daisy.

I'm looking for her now, I said.

She deserves the best, Daisy does, he said.

They were in the window embrasure when I found them. I'd come up quite close before they saw me. I thought at first they were talking about me.

I love him to death, Daisy was saying. There isn't a second

68

of the day I don't love him. I wake up in the night and I love him.

I sure hoped she was talking about me.

So what's the problem? Jack said. What's wrong. I don't see what's so difficult. If you love him, be with him. If you love him, call him. Call him now. Tell him you're coming home.

She wasn't talking about me.

Why don't you mind your own fucking business, I said.

Daisy didn't say anything. She sat and looked straight through me.

Just stay out of things that don't concern you, I said. Stick to your own life. Fuck that up if you like, but keep your hands off mine.

Baby! Jack said. Calm down. Stay cool.

Shit, I said. Stay cool. You should hear yourself.

Daisy stood up. Her face was scarlet.

Did you see Pip and Jim? she said. Jim said he should have something for you soon.

Daisy, I said.

Pip seems to like you, she said.

Lucky bastard, Jack said.

Daisy, I said. What is going on here? Something is going on here and I want to know what it is.

Didn't I tell you? Jack said. Cute but dumb.

Daisy, I said. Will you tell me what's going on?

Stay cool, baby, Jack said. Baby will hear when it's all ready. Baby must be patient.

I took a deep breath.

Right, I said. Fine. OK. Right. I'll just leave you to it then.

I turned to Daisy.

If I were you, I said, I should call Florida. Since that is so obviously what you want to do. Just sit right down now, and call him. I need another drink.

I would have stalked off if I could, but I turned round and bumped into Bella who had come up behind me.

Bella, I said. Let's go and have a drink. Let's go and have a dance. Let's go and party.

OK, she said.

Let's begin with the drink, I said.

But when we got to the piano all we could find was empty bottles so we danced instead. The room had thinned out. Here and there people sat on the floor. The odd couple smooched on the dancefloor to the croon of Brenda Lee. I took Bella round the waist and drew her towards me. She put her arms round my neck and rested her head on my shoulder and we swayed.

You're beautiful, Bella, I said. You're lovely. Hold me, Bella, I said. I need to be held. Jesus, Bella, I said. I can't bear it. I simply can't bear it.

She lifted her face and I kissed her.

What's the matter with me, Bella? I said.

It's not your fault, she said. You can't help it. It's just the way you are.

I kissed her again. She let me for a while and then she moved her head away.

You're just negative, she said. You're a negative person.

I stood stock still. She was going to say it. I knew she was going to say it. She said it.

I mean, you're good-looking . . . she said.

Oh God.

Look out when they say you're good-looking. It's the kiss of death when they say you're good-looking. It means they don't love you. You're a good-looking guy, they say. You could get anyone, they mean. You could have anyone. Just not me.

. . . but you don't do anything, she said. You aren't anything. You're just negative.

Jesus, Bella, I thought. Negative. You bovine bag. You blank, bland, boring, beautiful, bovine bag. *I'm* negative.

I took her head and laid it on my shoulder. I started swaying to Brenda Lee again. 'Johnny-One-Time'.

Jesus, Bella, I said. Talk about cute but dumb.

Her body swayed with mine. We danced till the music ended.

I'd better get back to Jack, she said. And you should find Daisy.

Yes, I said. I guess I should.

We found them in the kitchen. Jack was sitting on the table. Daisy was at the sink, drying mugs, beside her a teapot, milk and a steaming kettle.

Another good one, Jack said.

A grand one, Bella said.

Daisy wouldn't look at me.

Tea? she said.

You're a good woman, Jack said. Isn't she a grand woman, Bella?

Daisy took two more mugs from the draining board and added another spoonful to the pot.

I'd love some, I said.

Daisy still wouldn't look at me.

And hasn't she a grand man? Jack said. Daisy, come here and talk to your grand man.

He leaned across the table and caught Daisy's hand, pulling her over to him.

You're a lucky girl to have him, he said. He's a grand man. We love him, Bella and I. Don't we, Bella?

We do, Bella said.

He's a pretty man, he said. Isn't he a pretty man, Bella?

Jack, I said.

He was still holding Daisy's hand.

Shall I show you? he said. Will I show you how pretty the man is?

He took Daisy's hand and pressed it to his groin.

That's how pretty he is, he said. Isn't it, Bella?

Daisy looked at me.

She smiled.

Slowly, gracefully, gloriously, oh my darling Daisy, she smiled.

Daisy, I said. I love you, Daisy. Let's go home. Please take me home.

Jack let go Daisy's hand.

We went home.

THREE

I slept on Daisy's shoulder in the taxi. We arrived at Holland Park, and propped each other up the stairs. We barely had the strength to undress.

The slam of a door woke me. I had no idea what time it was. I leaped out of bed. I was alone. My mouth was ash-dry. I tried to shout out. My limbs ached. I couldn't make a sound. A peacock in the park shrieked. My skin felt like hot paper. I was alone. Where the fuck was Daisy? I tried to shout again and this time managed a croak. My head felt like a swollen bubble. I fell towards the door and as I pulled it open a flood of sour liquid filled my mouth.

Daisy! I yelled. Daisy! Where are you? Daisy?

The bathroom door opened and she was there.

Daisy, I said. You weren't there. I woke up and you weren't there.

She took me in her arms.

I thought you'd gone, I said. I thought you'd gone.

She held me.

No, she said. No. No. I haven't gone.

I woke up, I said. And you weren't there.

I'm here, she said. I haven't gone. I'm still here.

She let me go.

Come on, she said. Back to bed.

Don't go, I said.

Go back to bed, she said. I'm still here.

Don't leave me alone, I said.

A girl has to go to the bathroom, she said. Come on. Go back to bed. You feel hot. I'll bring you some water.

I love you, Daisy, I said. I really do love you, you know. You know that, Daisy. I love you.

She took me back to the bedroom, put me on the bed and flicked the sheet over me.

Just lie still, she said. It'll be all right now.

I smiled.

I'll get you a glass of water and you'll feel better, she said.

I closed my eyes.

Give me a kiss, I said.

She kissed my eyes.

She went to fetch some water.

I slept.

I woke with the sun in my eyes, God knows how much later, and she wasn't there. I had a drink from the glass of water she'd left on the bedside table and went back to sleep.

She wasn't there when I woke again at eleven o'clock either and there was a note under the water glass.

I thought, the note said, *I'd let you sleep. I've gone to see Mason. I'll spend the morning with him and I expect we'll have lunch. A few bits of dreary to get out of the way this afternoon. Don't cook anything. I'll be back by six and we'll go out.*

> *All my love,*
> *Daisy.*

I put the note back under the glass. I de-coked my eyes, and de-bagged my face. I showered and dressed – just a blue vest and running shorts – and took my hangover off to the park. I thought I'd walk for a while, maybe sit for a bit, have a gallon or two of tea at the café, and then head off to the King's Road to buy Daisy another present.

I arrived at the park at the same time as a great wave of children. There must have been thirty of them swirling about my ankles, all with picnic lunches in bright plastic bags. They didn't know what do at first. They stood stolid and silent and looked around, holding on hard to their bags. Then, one by one, and two by two, they melted into the gardens and I was alone under the trees.

It was, I decided, a lovely day, the sky a blue dome, deliciously cool in the walks, baking out on the grass. I walked to and through the formal garden by the tea shop thinking that flowers were balm to the queasy soul, and round to the bird part. The peacocks were all, or seemed to be, in moult. Not a long feather to be seen except where, here and there, the sun caught an eye in the grass.

The birds all stepped up to the fence to see if I had any scraps, and stepped away again when they found I hadn't. I went and sat by the fountain, where I decided that playing water, not flowers, was balm to the queasy soul. Despite the fact that the basin was full of weed and Coke cups and someone had thrown a pair of frilly knickers on to the fountain. There was somebody there to clean it, but he got on my nerves somehow, the way he just fished out the weed and left the Coke cups behind. The way he parked his wheelbarrow, walked to the other side of the basin, scooped up a languid forkful of weed and strolled back to the barrow, the way he left those damn-fool knickers flickering and dripping . . . Well, it irritated me all to hell, and I had to get out of there. Definitely time for a cup of tea.

Just behind the tea shop, by the statue of a boy playing with a bear (the one that looks as if he's playfully guiding the bear's snout up his ass) I saw the white peacock. It wasn't in moult. It was sitting up to its middle in a freshly weeded patch of earth, having a dirt bath.

It pitched and twitched in the earth. It wriggled in the cool dirt. I got up quite close – I could have leaned forward and touched it – before it jumped up, shook itself and walked away.

So who the hell was Mason? It struck me as I was queuing for my tea, up to my knees in children again.

77

What flavour would you like? the waiter asked the child in front of me. Strawberry, chocolate or vanilla?

The child looked at him, and looked at me, and crumpled up her face to cry.

I crouched down.

Pink, white or brown? I said.

The child uncrumpled her face.

A lolly, she said.

So we got that sorted out.

I didn't know any Mason. Daisy had never mentioned a Mason. I thought maybe I'd go across to Putney. I'd go to Antiquarius and buy Daisy a pot, and see how Bella was getting on after the party.

I bought my tea and took it outside. As I was drinking it, the lollipop child came and held my leg. A tanned, tow-mopped girl of around four, wearing nothing but a pair of Marks and Spencer underpants, she held my knee, and spread her sticky lolly over her face, and my thigh.

Hi, I said.

She wouldn't look at me.

I'm Peter-Patrick, I said. How are you? Isn't it a lovely day?

She still wouldn't look at me. She patted her lollipop on my knee, and pointed. I followed her finger out of the tea-park shade, and gasped. The white peacock was standing head-on, head up, tall as Lucifer, in the formal garden, a pillar of blazing white among the pinks, blues and domestic reds. I held my teacup hard to stop my hands shaking and put it very gently in its saucer.

We looked and looked, the lollipop child and I, until the bird ducked its head, turned and trailed its tail away and I could breathe again.

Well, well, I said.

The lollipop child looked at me now.

Thank you, I said. That was lovely. Thank you very much.

She pursed her lips and nodded, patted her lollipop one last time on my knee and stomped off.

My head ached. A drowsy numbness pained my senses. I wished to hell I hadn't left my dark glasses at home.

I bought two more cups of tea. After I'd drunk them I felt a bit better and went to the Gents to wash the traces of the lollipop child from my leg.

Ordinarily, I don't like children all that much.

My eyes were beginning to burn, so there was something else I'd left at home. Clearly I would have to stop off at a chemist's on my way to the King's Road to buy some drops, and why not a new pair of dark glasses while I was about it? It's always the same with a hangover. Everything is so far away that you can't think about it. You stand for ages dithering and flustering, till eventually you lose patience and march straight out leaving God knows what behind. Never the chequebook though, somehow. Some remnant of a guardian spirit always lets you lay your hand on that.

There wasn't much of a choice at my usual stall at Antiquarius, but what choice there was was so great that I couldn't get my mind round it at all. I mean, I quickly got it narrowed down to two, but those two were both so totally right that I couldn't decide.

One was a Clarice Cliff vase, all foxgloves and sunlight and the outline of trees. The other was a big round jug by Charlotte Rhead, with a knotted wistaria branch against a crepuscular blue. So tell me, which would you have chosen?

I was within a hair's breadth of taking them both but managed to stop myself. They were both well on the far side of a hundred pounds. I moithered and dickered, walked away round the market and walked back. I tried to find something else. I tried to decide to go somewhere else. But by now the choice between the two pots was so lodged in my head that I couldn't grasp anything else. Seems familiar, huh?

In the end I cut the knot by closing my eyes and grabbing. My hand landed on the Charlotte Rhead, so I said, This one. Wrap it. Quick. And take the other one away. Just get it out of my sight. God, but it's beautiful, though. No, take it away. Quickly now, and let me get out of here.

All the way to Putney I had to fight the urge to open the parcel. I knew that if I did I'd wish I'd bought the Clarice Cliff. I wished I'd bought the Clarice Cliff anyway but I knew that if I opened the parcel I'd have to get the taxi to turn round and take me back and the whole thing would start all over again. I sat the parcel on my lap, and stared firmly out of the window.

Which was why, on Putney Bridge, I saw Grey-flannels sitting in the back of another taxi heading in the same direction as mine. I drew back hastily into the other corner but he'd seen me and started smiling and waving, so I had to lean forward again and smile and wave back. His taxi drew ahead of mine and I wondered where he was going, until it became apparent that not only were we heading in the same direction, we were going to the same street. I told my driver to drop me at the corner of Combemartin Road and watched Grey-flannels get out of his taxi outside Bella's house and go and knock on the door. The door opened and he went in.

I went and sat on a garden wall under a moiré tree, and waited.

There used to be a moiré tree at my home in the country when I was young. I don't know what the real name is. I'm not good with trees. I'm pretty sure it's an acacia, or an azalea, or something like that. If I'd had my wits about me I'd never have sat under it.

It's a confusing tree. Its leaves are a sort of smoky green colour that seems to float out beyond the actual body of the tree into a sort of blurred and blurring halo that gets behind the eyes. And the shape of the leaves is such that, layered over each other as they are, they form a moiré, a dancing reticulation of pluses and minuses that dislocates your vision, clouds your senses and subtracts what wits you have left from a burning hangover until you simply can't think straight at all.

I didn't want to think much, actually. I didn't want to think of why Grey-flannels was visiting Bella, of how maybe if her neck muscles were taut under his touch, it wasn't revulsion they were taut with. That I didn't want to think about.

But I did think about it. I sat under the moiré tree for an hour, an hour and a half, two hours, until Grey-flannels came out of the house and walked away down the street and I could get up and out from under the net. Even then I remembered, half-way to Bella's door, that I'd left the Charlotte Rhead on the wall, and I had to go back and get it.

I was in a bit of a state when I finally reached the house and Bella, without waiting for me to knock, opened the door and walked back down the corridor to the sitting room without saying a word.

She didn't need to. She was barefoot, clearly naked under a tattered red and black kimono with a golden dragon embroidered on the back that wriggled and coiled as she walked and a ripped and draggled hem with the padding falling out.

I followed her into the sitting room.

Well, she said. This is a surprise.

No attempt had been made to clear up the room. The stink of cigarettes and stale booze made my stomach rise. The piano was a mess of bottles, its white sheet cover striped and spattered with variegated stains. Fragments of fruit were trodden into the carpet.

Bella opened a window.

I've not had time to clean, she said. What with one thing and another. I'm sure you won't mind. Sit down, why don't you?

I sat down. On the sofa. Next to an overflowing ashtray.

Jack's not here, Bella said.

It isn't Jack I've come to see, I said.

Is it not? she said.

No, I said. Bella, you know it isn't.

I know what I know, she said. I know how much time you spend together. I know what you do when you are together. I'm a bit of a fool, I know. But I'm not blind.

She sat on the windowsill. She hoisted her feet up under her buttocks, clasped her hands round her knees, and leaned back into the tightened sag of the net curtains.

The sun shone behind her.

Will you have a cup of tea or something? she said.

No, I said. No thanks.

Something to eat maybe, she said. A piece of toast? Some bacon and eggs? Breakfast?

No thanks, I said. No.

We sat. I on the sofa. She on the windowsill. She craned her head down and rubbed her finger between her toes. I felt my cock inch up my belly into an erection. There isn't much you can do to hide an erection in a pair of running shorts. I put the Charlotte Rhead parcel between my legs.

I don't mind or anything, she said. About you and Jack. It doesn't worry me.

Well, I said. It sure as hell worries me. I didn't ask for it. I don't want it. I don't want Jack. You know who I want.

Sure, I know who you want now, she said. I can see who you want now.

I shifted on the sofa.

Well, why not? I said. Just why the hell not?

She swung forward on the windowsill and jumped to her feet.

Why not indeed? she said. Which reason would you like first? What about the fact that I don't like you very much, will that do for starters? What about the fact that I like Daisy? What about my husband, who you've been screwing for months, and now you say you didn't even like it? Will that do, or do you want more?

Oh, why not let's have some more? I said. What about two in one afternoon? What about that fat grey whale you've spent the last two hours pleasuring? What about the God knows who you had last night? And this morning, don't let's forget this morning. By all means don't let's forget this morning. Who did you manage to cram in this morning. You sure as hell weren't clearing up this pigsty, that's obvious.

She was still standing by the window and the light shone round her.

Like! I said. Who cares if you like me or not? What's liking got to do with anything? You think I like your appalling husband when I fuck him every day? You think I like you? I don't like one tiniest part of you. I just can't get you out of my head, that's all. I just can't stop seeing you all the time between me and what I really want, what I really like. That's all.

I was panting.

That's all, I said. Nothing more. I want to get rid of you. I want you to go away. I want never to have to think about you or see you again.

She walked towards me out of the light. I wasn't sure what I was saying.

I want to forget you, I said. I want to forget that I ever knew you. I want to take you, hold you, fuck you and forget you. I want to burn you out of my body. I want to fuck you out of my mind.

She unloosed the kimono and stood in front of me. I couldn't look at her.

Oh God, I said.

She squatted between my legs.

Bella . . . I said.

I . . . I said.

She took the Charlotte Rhead parcel and put it on the floor by my feet.

Bella . . . I said.

She kissed my crotch through my running shorts. She ran her hands down my thighs. I sat bolt upright on the sofa, and gripped the back with my hands.

Jesus . . . Bella . . . I said.

And Jack came in.

Naked and yawning. Scratching his belly. A smoke of hair across his chest.

I pushed Bella back and stood up. She sat on the floor and laughed.

What's all the noise? Jack said.

Bella kicked the Charlotte Rhead parcel as she stood up. I picked it up.

Hi, I said.

Ah, Jack said. Company. Fetch us a towel to wrap round myself, Bella love.

Bella tied up her kimono and, still laughing, left.

I'll stay and entertain the guest, Jack said.

I just came . . . I said. I wanted . . . I was going to . . .

Seduce my wife, Jack said. Fuck my wife. Is what you came to do. Bof the consort. Bonk the spouse. Wop it up the little woman. Is what you came to do.

He put the tips of his fingers on my chest and pushed.

Jack, I said.

Don't give me that, he said.

He pushed my chest again.

Would you look at the man? he said. Just look at the man. All togged up in his Filas and his Nikes. Vested and shorted and short-socked for the pleasure of my wife.

He pushed me again.

I clenched my teeth.

Jack, I said.

And the parcel, he said. Would you look at the parcel? A love gift, is it? A little token for the boffee.

He took the parcel and pushed me with it. The sofa caught me behind the knees and I sat down.

That's right, Jack said. Make yourself comfortable. Make yourself at home. Take over the place, why don't you? Fucking me isn't enough for you, is that it? You have to fuck my wife on top of it. So let's have a look at the love gift then. Let's see what he thinks the wife is worth. Damn the thing he ever gave me.

It's not, I said. It's for Daisy. It's a present for Daisy.

Sure, he said.

He snapped the string. He ripped the paper off.

Sure it is, he said. You just happened to buy it on the way.

He took the pot out of the torn wrapping, and put it on the piano.

It's Daisy's, I said. It's Daisy's birthday present.

He picked up an empty bottle.

Yeah, yeah, he said. Of course it is. That and the tape recorder.

Jack, I said.

Of course it is, he said.

He hit the pot with the bottle.

Jack, I said.

He knocked the handle off.

Yeah, he said.

He smashed the bottle down on the jug, and broke it in pieces.

I threw myself at him. I punched him right in the mouth.

So, he said.

I stood in front of him with my fists clenched. I was trembling. My kneecaps were jigging up and down. My teeth chattered from sheer rage.

So, he said.

He flung a backhand across the side of my face.

We fought.

We clawed and hacked and grappled. We tore each other's hair and face. We stumbled. We tumbled. We clutched and punched and rolled. And the next thing I knew, he was sitting on top of me with his hand down my shorts.

I couldn't help myself.

You bastard, I said.

He held my cock.

You fucking bastard, I said. You fucking shit.

He fitted my cock into him.

So, he said.

You fucking, fucking, fucking bastard, I said.

Yeah, he said.

I tried to throw him off.

Oh no, he said.

I tried. I really tried. But I couldn't.

Oh no, he said. We won't have any of that. We do it. We do it all. And get it finished. Bella!

He shouted.

Jesus, I said. Jack. Jesus.

Bella! he shouted.

And there was Bella. Towel in hand. A riot of hair.

Oh God, I said.

Fuck him! Bella said.

She hit Jack with the towel. She thrashed him with the towel over the head, the back, the shoulders.

Fuck him! she shouted. Fuck him.

I fucked him.

I fucked him and it was finished.

And when it was finished, and Jack was towelling himself down, and Bella was patting her breasts back into her kimono, and I was straightening my clothes as best I could, Jack said, it would help. It really would. It wouldn't be quite so bad. If you could bring yourself even to pretend to enjoy it.

There didn't seem to be much I could say to that, so I finished straightening myself up and left.

I eventually got a taxi to stop for me on the Fulham side of Putney Bridge. I hadn't minded walking. I hadn't minded when the three taxis I had seen drove right on by. I was walking on air. I whistled in the back of the taxi that did stop for me. I told the driver to wait for me outside Antiquarius, where they looked at me pretty oddly as I bought the Clarice Cliff for Daisy, so I guess I must have looked a bit rough, but he'd gone when I got out. I really must have looked rough for him to have gone off without his fare. I didn't care. I walked till I got another one. And I walked home across Holland Park anyway.

It was six o'clock when I got home. Daisy let out a yelp when she saw me.

What's happened? she said. Where have you been? What have you done?

I hugged her.

Hello, Daisy, I said. Darling Daisy.

I tried to kiss her, but it hurt, so I picked her up and swung her round. That hurt too.

Daisy, I said. Daisy. Daisy.

It's all right, I said. Everything's all right. I'm all right. I ran into someone, that's all. I'm all right. I'm better now.

Daisy peeled off my clothes, and stood me in the shower. I watched the blood rinse off my body and down the drain. I laughed.

You are going to be black and blue, Daisy said. You are going to look a real mess. What on earth have you been doing?

I'd love a drink, I said. I want a drink and a dance and an enormous meal.

What you're going to do, she said, is have a bath. A good long soak. And a cup of hot sweet tea. And bed.

I jumped out of the shower and hugged her again. It really hurt this time, so I yelled and sat on the edge of the bath. That hurt too, so I stood up again.

Daisy ran the bath. I looked at myself in the mirror. My right eye was swollen, slit, and closed. My bottom lip was split, my top lip lop-sided and torn. I had three scratch marks down my left cheek. Daisy got some cotton wool and some witch hazel and swabbed my face. I hissed and winced.

God, I feel good, I said. I feel better now. It's been on my mind all summer and now it's gone. I feel cleaner. Cleaner.

Daisy turned off the bath taps, and dropped oil and salts into the water. They reacted with each other, and formed a sort of soapy sludge under the surface, but I didn't have the heart to tell her, so I got in and lay down, and she knelt by the edge as I soaked.

So? she said.

It's been on my mind all summer, I said. Nagging away quietly at the root of my mind. That business in the park. The bastard who broke my foot. Well, I saw him again today. By himself. All alone. And I followed him and thrashed him and evened the score, and I feel like a million dollars. A million fucking dollars. A million bloody, bloody dollars.

Suddenly I didn't feel so good after all. Suddenly I felt rather awful. I went cold under the bath water.

Daisy, I said.

She stood up.

It's all right, she said.

She fetched a towel.

Come on, she said. Out you get. It's all right.

I stood up. I was hot and cold at the same time.

It's all right, Daisy said. You'll be OK.

She wrapped me in the towel and I climbed out of the bath.

It always goes like this, she said. You'll be all right. Soon.

She held me.

All right soon, she said.

I couldn't move.

Come on, she said. Let's get you to bed.

No, I said. No.

You'll be all right, she said. It's always like this. Come on.

No, I said. I can't. No.

She held me. I stood there frozen in my towel and she held me. Then I felt all right again.

Jesus, I said. Jesus. That wasn't nice.

Come on, she said. Tea, like I told you. And bed.

The tea was disgusting. A great milky bowl of it, treacly sweet. I lay back against the pillows, and Daisy sat on the bed and made me drink it all. I had no strength to resist. I sipped, and grimaced, and sipped till it was all gone. Daisy took the bowl from my hands and I slept.

Light was glowing behind the curtains when I woke up and Daisy was curled up next to me, so I guessed it must be morning. I slipped from under the bedcover – well, maybe slipped isn't quite the right word. It began as a slip and was interrupted by a gigantic all-over body twinge. I hissed and moaned and damn near woke up Daisy, which wasn't the idea at all. She twitched, turned, and hugged the pillow, and I crept stiffly to the bathroom, where a glance in the mirror made me reach for my dressing gown.

I was purpling up nicely. A closer inspection told me that I didn't have to worry about my face. It was beyond repair. The right side a bulging hemisphere, brown and black and mauve, the eye all but invisible in the wadded flesh. The left a rather horrible yellow, with three bright ruby-crusted nail stripes down the cheek. I shrugged – not without pain – my shoulders. Fuck it, I thought. It was worth it. And I went into the kitchen to fix a special birthday breakfast. A grapefruit, champagne, smoked salmon and scrambled eggs, and a rose from the balcony.

I wrapped the Clarice Cliff parcel in festal paper, fetched the musical suitcase and the tapes from the wardrobe, and put them round Daisy's sleeping form on the bed. I half opened the curtains and was going to get the breakfast tray when I saw Daisy's face on the pillow in the morning light and had to stop.

Her hair was looped back and her muscles were relaxed in sleep. The usual slender oval of her face sagged. Her mouth was open, her cheek drooped on to the pillow and a trail of spittle dropped from her lip. Her eyes were sunken, the sockets puffy and lined. There was the distinct promise of a double chin, and you could see the scalp through her hair. Her skin was slicked over with grease.

I went up to the bed, leaned over her face, which I hadn't realized till that moment was middle-aged, and was buffeted by such a wave of fondness that I nearly fell across her. I caught myself, kissed her hair and went to get the breakfast tray.

Daisy, I said. Daisy. Happy birthday. Wake up.

I put the tray on the bedside table. She opened her eyes and I twitched and scraped like Quasimodo.

I'll go away, I said. So you don't have to see my ugly face while you're eating.

She sat up and I plumped the pillows behind her. She looked at her parcels and at me.

Your poor face, she said.

Why was I not made of stone, I said. Like thee.

She laughed.

Eat, I said. Straightaway. Now. Before it gets cold.

I forked up some salmon and egg and held it to her mouth.

All of it now, I said. Eat it all up.

She took the food from the fork.

Delicious, she said. Just perfect.

And the champagne, I said.

She sipped.

Lovely, she said. What are you having?

I thought I'd have a bit of yours, I said.

She piled some salmon and egg on to a sliver of toast and I ate it.

Oh, I said. Ow. It hurts. But you're right, I said. It's delicious.

Champagne? she said.

You bet, I said. You don't think I'm going to let you drink the whole bottle by yourself.

We clinked our glasses together.

To us, I said.

Happy birthday to me, she said.

A wire of pain flickered in my football cheek and my ear sang.

We drank. We finished breakfast. I fetched Daisy's camera and took photographs of her opening her presents, of her surrounded by piles of brightly coloured paper, of her cradling her Clarice Cliff pot. You try taking photographs with your left eye.

It's lovely, she said. It's really lovely.

Well, you had to have a surprise, I said. And you guessed the radio.

She sat and hugged the pot.

It's lovely, she said.

Isn't it? I said.

She hung her head over the pot.

I don't know what to say, she said.

No need to say anything, I said.

Her hair slipped out of its knot and fell down around the pot. I brushed it back and raised her head.

Nowhere near, I said, nowhere near as lovely as my Daisy. Not even sort of. Not even close.

She blinked.

Your poor face, she said.

I brushed her lips with the uninjured side of my mouth.

Never mind the face, I said. You should see my poor body.

I nuzzled her cheek. Very carefully she took my face in her hands.

I must get up, she said. I must wash and scrub my face and bath.

I turned my face and kissed the palm of her hand.

Happy birthday, Daisy, I said.

I kissed her hand again.

My Daisy, I said. Off you go. I'll clear up this.

My ear was still singing. Swallowing in a certain way, using the throat and the base of the nose, interrupted the pain I found, and I swallowed again and again as I gathered up the paper and string and straightened the pillows and bedcover. I bundled the pile of paper into the bin in the kitchen and I washed up the breakfast things. The pitch of the singing in my ear rose and fell and rose again, until pretty soon no sort of swallowing had any effect on it and I couldn't bear it.

I stuck my little finger in and jiggled. The pain was immediate and intense. It was as if a flower of pain had bloomed in my ear, sending roots over my skull and down my back. It was as if something had exploded in my head. I cringed.

But the singing, and eventually the pain, stopped. I went back to the bedroom, fully opened the curtains and gave myself over to the problem of what clothes showed off to best advantage my new multi-coloured features.

I had just about decided, well almost just about decided, on monochrome black – baggy T-shirt, with even baggier cotton overshirt not tucked into cotton trousers, the sort with pleats at the front, and loafers (no socks – I love the look of naked feet thrust into loafers), when my ear closed. It was as if someone had held a pillow against it. Or pulled a blind in my head. There was a sort of frilly whrump and that was it.

It happens to me occasionally. Usually it's a build-up of wax in my ear that blocks it off. This time, I imagined, it was some sort of inner bruising or swelling that had inflamed the tissues and closed the channel. It's a sensation I detest, a blocked ear. I usually take precautions against it – a few bicarbonate of soda drops from time to time – but this one I was clearly going to have to put up with.

Half-unconsciously I raised my hand as if to jiggle with my little finger again, but as soon as I caught sight of what I was doing in the mirror I knew I wouldn't be able to do it. Simply bringing my finger close to my ear made me feel sick with pain. Sod it, I thought. Just the thing to really help me make Daisy have a good birthday. This is really going to help.

Like I said, I can't think of a sensation I dislike more than a blocked ear. It's worse even than toothache. Because all a toothache does is hurt. A blocked ear – even just one blocked ear – whether it hurts you or not, puts you in prison. It locks you inside your head. You hear everything from the inside. Your voice, amplified, rough, clogged and hoarse. The furry pulse of blood in your ears. The rush of air through your face as you breathe. The chomp and gulp of mastication. Even the pivot of your skull on its vertebrae as you turn your head. All exaggeratedly and continually audible, drowning out all other sound, inducing a maddening feeling of separation, of isolation inside yourself.

I really don't like it.

As if the day weren't going to be big enough without that.

I really wanted Daisy to enjoy her birthday. I wanted her to be happy. I wanted – free of Bella, free of Jack, even with a gaudy football for a face – I wanted to make her happy.

I needed my wits about me.

I brought my finger up again to my ear but it was no good. I shook my head, slightly at first, then a bit harder, but all I got was a sort of bubbling throb. I shook harder still, and got an aching roar, a roaring ache, and I knew that that was no good either. I was just going to have to put up with it. I transferred my attention back to my clothes. I put on the black outfit and saw at once that it wouldn't do.

It took me a long time to work out why. I twisted and turned in front of the mirror trying to work out why. I mean, there was nothing wrong with the outfit. It hung together perfectly. It went beautifully with my battered face, in a bully-boy, Jack Palance sort of way. But there was a spark missing. I tried it with the overshirt tucked into the trousers. I tried it with the T-shirt pulled out of the trousers. You can always tell when you have the look right. You look in the mirror and you feel a spark in your groin, the beginnings of an erection. It's a sure sign. And if the spark's not there, forget it. Remember that the next time you go shopping. It'll save you many an expensive mistake. And like I said, the spark wasn't there. I couldn't find it. And I couldn't see why.

Or at least I couldn't until I looked away out of the mirror to the window and saw that it was the world that had changed, not I. The light had changed.

It wasn't summer any more.

I went out on to the balcony and sniffed the air. The wind blew over the park, through the tops of the trees and a leaf blew off here and there. It wasn't cold, but it wasn't hot either. The sky was full of scudding clouds and the balcony door slammed shut behind me. I leaned on the parapet and watched the surge of the wind through the trees. I love autumn. The languid season. Season of easy melancholy and peaceful decline. But I love even more the first days of late summer when the air is full of the promise of autumn, when the clear light of summer takes on a sort of watery density, when a young man's fancy lightly turns from meditation on the sere and yellow leaf to thoughts of winter clothes.

I toyed with the idea of navy blue trousers and a blue cotton pullover and then I thought, To hell with it, I'll go the whole hog. I'll go forward into the future with open arms. I'll go for full autumn.

So back I went to the wardrobe. I looked out brown suede brogues, chocolate brown socks, bottle green corduroy trousers, a rust-coloured turtleneck pullover over a cream shirt with a brown neck-scarf. And when I looked in the mirror, there was the spark all right. It looked fabulous. All I needed was a tweed cap and a stout stick. My face made me look as if I was recovering from a hunting accident.

I let out a whoop of success that echoed in my blocked ear, made my jaw ache and brought Daisy in from the bathroom, so I could see that she had had the same idea. We looked at each other and laughed. Her hair was up under a tweed hat, which she had pulled down over one eye, and a pheasant feather. A tightly waisted, broad-shouldered, pencil-skirted suit of lovat green houndstooth tweed, with a slit up the back of the skirt. The creamiest of silk blouses with an enormous jabot at the throat. Stockings with seams. And sensible shoes. Like I said, we looked at each other and at ourselves and we laughed. We stood side by side in front of the mirror and she took my arm.

We belong together, I said.

She leaned her tweed-hatted head lightly on my shoulder.

Like a stamp to a letter, she said.

I blew her pheasant feather away from my nose.

Like a horse and carriage, I said.

We decided to walk across the park to have lunch. Daisy had chosen the restaurant, a little place she knew, where for the price of a small car two waistline-conscious people could eat without fear. We hadn't been out ten minutes before it became obvious that our simultaneous autumnal mood had been a bit previous. The wind dropped and soon we were sweltering in our heavy clothes. Daisy took off her hat and jacket, and let down her hair. I took off my pullover and let the neck-scarf hang loose, but I still sweated. Daisy, of course, looked poised and cool, ever so slightly *dégagée*, and beautiful as always. Heads turned to look at us when we arrived at the restaurant. Wherever you go with Daisy heads turn.

More champagne, I said as we sat down. More champagne for the birthday girl.

A half bottle, Daisy said.

A half bottle! I said. No way. A bottle. Two bottles.

I mustn't get too drunk, she said. I should work this afternoon.

Work, I said. You can't work. It's your birthday. What could you possibly have to do on your birthday? Nobody works on their birthday.

Just a little, she said. I've still got a few details to see to. A few last minute things to run through with Mason.

The waiter arrived with the champagne, and made a business of setting up the ice bucket next to the table.

Mason? I said when he'd gone. Who is this Mason? What is all this Mason business?

Just business, Daisy said. Just ordinary everyday sort of business. Nothing special. Pour the champagne.

I poured.

Yes, I said. But who's Mason?

She lifted her glass.

Don't be silly, she said. You met him. At Jack and Bella's party. You know him. Everyone knows Mason.

I raised my glass.

Ah well, I said. Happy birthday. Long life to you.

We drank.

Long life to us, I said.

We drank again.

And perdition to Jack and Bella, I said.

95

Daisy giggled into her glass.

Wasn't it awful? she said. Wasn't it the worst? Wasn't it just the worst party you've ever been to?

Oh easily, I said. Positively.

I took a sip of champagne.

I don't think, I said, we'll be seeing so much of them from now on. I think that party represented some sort of climax. Anyway I don't think I could go through all that again.

Oh, they were OK, Daisy said. A bit out of the ordinary maybe, but OK. The heart was in the right place. They had a soft spot for you.

I laughed. I had to laugh. I noted the past tense but I had to laugh.

They had a soft spot for me all right, I said. Oh yes.

I lifted my glass.

Oh yes, I said. Well, fuck them. Fuck them and their soft spot for me. I don't know what I did to deserve their soft spot for me.

My ear buzzed. I was hot as hell. Daisy lifted her glass.

The important thing to remember, she said, is that they've done it before. This is nothing new. Like with the man who broke your foot. If someone behaves to you in a certain way, then they've behaved in that way to someone else before. You're simply the latest in a long line of people they've behaved like that to. It isn't personal. It isn't you. They make a habit of it.

Cheers, I said.

Like love, Daisy said. Just like with love. If someone falls for you in a certain way, it's because they've made a habit of falling in that way before. You're simply the latest in a long line of people they've fallen for in that way.

Daisy, I said. You're talking nonsense. Who's talking about love? We're talking about two tacky people who throw dreary and messy parties and lead dreary and messy lives. And I for one am glad to be shot of them.

Just a general point, she said. A girl is allowed to be philosophical on her birthday.

I waved my champagne glass.

Cheers? I said.

I wish you hadn't done it, she said.

What? I said. You wish I hadn't done what?

Gone and got yourself knocked around, she said. Was it worth it? Putting yourself in danger. Spoiling your face.

Rather an abrupt change of subject, I said, isn't it? We were talking about Jack and Bella.

I put my glass down.

It comes to the same thing, she said. He was doing just what they were. I don't see the point of it. Getting yourself beaten up for someone who doesn't really see you. Someone you're just another piece of a pattern for. I don't think you should have done it.

Daisy, I said. You don't know the half of it. What do you mean you don't think I should have done it? I don't see that I couldn't have done it. It was worth it. Believe me, it was worth it. I felt dirty and now I feel clean. How could it not be worth it?

I picked up my glass again.

Now let's not talk about it any more, I said. Let's have our drink and our lunch, and let's get on with what really matters. Let's get on with your birthday.

Cheers, she said.

Perdition to Jack and Bella, she said. Perdition to the man who broke your foot and spoiled your face. Long life to us.

We drank and I refilled the glass.

It isn't anyway, I said. Is it? Spoiled. My face. Well only temporarily.

She laughed. She spluttered into her glass.

Oh, Peter-Patrick, she said. Don't ever change. Promise me you won't ever change.

I looked at the table.

Daisy stopped laughing. She reached across the table and held my hand.

I'm sorry, she said. It's just . . .

Yeah, I said. I know.

Peter-Patrick, she said. I really am sorry.

Yeah, I said. I'm a silly boy. You're a woman of the world. And you're sorry.

Sorrier than you know, she said. It's my birthday after all.

She let go my hand and picked up her glass.

Come on, she said. Show a lady a good time.

We finished the bottle.

God I'm hot in all this gear, I said.

I shifted in my chair to ungum my corduroys from my skin. I undid another shirt buttom. My ear stopped buzzing and started fizzing. I looked at the menu. It was all seaweed, shad's roe, kiwi fruit and raspberry vinegar.

Do you know, I said. Just for once I should like to eat something really fattening.

Fish and chips, Daisy said.

Macaroni cheese, I said.

Lemon meringue pie, she said.

Deep-fried Camembert, I said.

Christmas pudding and brandy butter, she said.

Deep-fried Christmas pudding and brandy butter, I said.

Then the waiter came, and I ordered a carrot and orange soup and a steamed dover sole with a green salad.

Daisy really pushed the boat out and ordered a crab mousse and a *salade tiède* of mangetout and chicken livers.

I ordered another bottle of champagne and by the time it and the meal were finished things were getting a bit on top of me. What with my face, my ear, the heat, the wine and all. I went to the lavatory to get myself reorganized.

I pulled out and undid my shirt. I undid my trousers, kicked off my shoes and went and sat in a cubicle. My feet left foot-shaped patches of condensation on the cool grey floortiles. My blood whistled through my undamaged ear and shrieked through the blocked one.

I leaned my head back against the cistern, let my stomach sag, and blew through my mouth. Pretty soon I was cooler. I buttoned up and tucked in and forced my feet back into my still smouldering shoes. I washed my face and noticed too late that the place was too hi-tech to have a towel so I had to use the hot-air machine, and went back into the restaurant. I didn't look in the mirror once. It's a game I have. To see if I can do it.

There is a way you can tell, when you see them from behind, if someone is crying. Don't ask me how precisely, but you can tell. Obviously not the full shoulder-quaking, head-shaking crying jag. You don't have to be a master of observation to recognize that from any angle. But something about the slope of her shoulders, the tilt of her head, told me as I walked up behind her to get back to our table that Daisy was either having a quiet cry, or trying hard not to.

It annoyed me rather, actually.

It annoyed the shit out of me, to tell you the truth.

I mean, I was trying. I was really trying. I was carting about my aching body for her. I was suffering in silence about my goddamn ear for her – and suffering in silence is not something I'm good at unless it's been made fairly clear somewhere along the line that that is what I'm doing. I was giving her as good a time as I knew how.

I thought it was plain tactless of her to be crying.

When I rounded the table and sat down she gave me a brave, biting-back-the-tears sort of smile. I could have slapped her.

Phew, I said. That's better.

It was Jasper, of course. It just had to be Jasper. You see Daisy looking soulful and weepy, and it's bound to be Jasper.

Had enough? I said. Shall we go home?

She smiled bravely again. I hate it when people smile bravely. Why the hell didn't she just telephone the little brat if that's what she wanted so goddamn much? I don't see what's the big deal. So she's not supposed to see him. She can talk to him every now and again, can't she? It wouldn't kill anyone for her to talk to him, would it?

Or we could have a coffee, I said. Would you like a coffee?

99

She shook her head.

I couldn't stand it. If she didn't stop soon I was going to say something. To give her time to snap out of it, I made a business of calling the waiter and asking for the bill, and by the time I'd paid it I was relieved to see that she had succeeded.

He hadn't even sent her a birthday card, after all.

We walked home.

The autumnal feel of the morning had definitely worn off by the time we reached Holland Park, and it was as hot as midsummer. It didn't seem to affect Daisy. She had her coat over her shoulders, carried her hat and swung along. Not me. I undid more and more buttons on my shirt till eventually I pulled it out of my trousers and let it flap open. I knotted my pullover round my hips.

Daisy, I said. Slow down. It isn't a marathon. Let's just walk.

The park was full. People on blankets everywhere. Radios and frisbee players.

We walked past the tea shop, through the formal garden to the bird section, and leaned, with a crowd of other people, on the fence to look at the birds. They were all on the far side of the area sitting in the shade, except for one who was standing by the fence, spreading his tail for all he was worth.

It wasn't much of a tail. He was in moult and all he had was his base feathers and the odd long one here and there, but he wasn't allowing that to bother him. He shook and turned as if he was flaring his full complement. Everyone was laughing. My neighbour on the fence chuckled and dug me in the ribs. I jumped.

Just look at him, he said. Don't he look a mess? Don't he look a bleeding mess, eh?

He dug me in the ribs again. I yelped.

Sorry mate, he said. Didn't see you was hurt. What a sight, eh?

I didn't answer.

It was the man who'd broken my foot.

I nearly choked.

He was shorter than I remembered, and dirtier, and younger. He must have been about sixteen. His hair was cropped to the skin and he wore rolled-up jeans and Doc Marten's boots with steel toecaps. The front of his T-shirt was pulled up behind his head so that it bunched over his shoulders and showed a massive tattoo on his chest. It was a fine piece of work in red and blue and green. It stretched from his navel to his throat, from nipple to nipple. It was a peacock in full display.

Been in the wars, eh? he said.

I cleared my throat.

Ah, I said. Yes. You should see the other guy.

Yeah, he said. I know what you mean. What a mess, eh?

Daisy leaned round me to look at him.

Hi, she said.

'Lo, he said. What a mess, eh?

Daisy looked at the peacock.

He does look a bit shabby, she said.

Don't he, though, the skinhead said.

He chuckled again.

Bird don't look too hot neither, he said.

Daisy laughed. I laughed too. It seemed appropriate.

Funny old birds, the skinhead said.

Daisy pointed at his chest.

You obviously like them, she said.

Sure do, he said. Yeah. I like them. They're good.

We all looked at the bird.

People think it's sex, the skinhead said.

It didn't sound as if there was anything wrong with his tongue.

It isn't though, he said. That with the tail. You see it in the chicks. Just out of the egg. All small and bald and that. They wriggle up their backs just the same. Can't tell me that's sex.

It doesn't sound like it, Daisy said. You know a lot about them.

Yeah, he said. I like them. I read books about them. I come here all the time to look at them. They're good.

The bird stamped and preened in his tatters.

Daft bugger, the skinhead said. What a bleedin' mess, eh?

He looked at me.

Sure is, I said.

Seen you before, haven't I, he said.

I looked at the bird. I presented him with my battered profile.

It's possible, I said.

Sure I've seen you before, he said.

Hard to tell behind all the bruises, I said.

He comes here often too, Daisy said. He comes to look at the birds too. I expect you saw him then.

I reached my hand forward and clucked at the peacock. It ignored me.

No, the skinhead said. You don't do it like that. You got to do it like this.

He pursed his lips and sucked a thin hiss through them. The bird stood still, then shook his feathers. The skinhead hissed again and the bird put down his tail.

There, the skinhead said.

Very good, I said.

Eat out of my fingers too, it will, the skinhead said. Not many people he'd do that for. See.

Again he hissed. The bird turned its head from side to side and took a step forward. The skinhead took a much scrumpled Yorkie bar from his back pocket and nipped off a corner which he held out to the bird. He raised the pitch of his hiss and broke it by tapping his tongue against his teeth. Gingerly the bird tiptoed forward. The skinhead changed his hiss for a sort of fluting mew and the bird, its head turned almost sideways, tweeked the chocolate from his fingers with its beak.

There, the skinhead said. How about that? Isn't that great?

That was great, Daisy said. That was lovely.

The skinhead looked at her.

Seen you too, he said. I seen you both before.

I shrugged.

It's possible, I said. We get around.

We both live near here, Daisy said. We come here all the time. I expect that's what it is.

The skinhead looked from me to Daisy and back again with narrowed eyes.

Yeah, he said. 'Spect so. S'pose so.

He transferred his attention back to the bird.

He hissed again and clicked with his tongue, and the bird shook its feathers. I turned to Daisy.

OK? I said.

The bird spread out a wing and stretched it.

OK, Daisy said.

Daft bugger, the skinhead said.

Daisy held out her hand to him.

We have to go now, she said.

They shook hands.

Been nice talking to you, he said. 'Spect I'll see you round here again. Seeing as we both come and look at the birds.

I expect so, Daisy said.

I nodded at him.

Have a good day, I said.

Bye now, he said.

The peacock raised its tail and the skinhead turned away and started hissing and clicking at it again.

The trouble with you, Daisy said, slipping an arm round my waist under my shirt as we walked across the lawn and down the rose walk towards Lord Holland's statue.

Yes, I said. Yes? The trouble with me. What's the trouble with me?

You're a snob, Daisy said. You hardly spoke to that boy. You hardly even looked at him. You were lofty and chilly. It's possible! Very good! Have a good day! You were on the verge of telling him he probably recognized us from the television, weren't you? Go on. Weren't you?

Not exactly, I said. Not quite.

She laughed.

Oh yes you were, she said. I could feel it.

Well, so what if I was, I said. It's true, isn't it?

She laughed again.

Isn't it? I said.

Oh yes, she said. It's true all right.

Well then, I said. I guess I must be a snob then. I s'pose. I 'spect. One thing's for sure. I'll never be able to look at the peacocks in the same light again.

I hissed and clicked my tongue. Daisy squeezed my waist.

Daft bugger, she said.

We both laughed this time. Daisy let go my waist and took my hand.

It was true, though. The peacocks would never be the same again. I would never be able to enjoy them in the same way again. They had been spoiled. I could feel the loss of them slowly growing, like a hole in my stomach, as we walked home.

The first thing Daisy did when we arrived, before I had shut the door even, before she took her shoes off even, was take off her skirt. She unzipped it and kicked if off in the hall, shrugged off her jacket, kicked off her shoes and went out on to the balcony in her blouse and tights. Through the window I saw her take off the rest of her clothes and stand with her arms outstretched to let what wind there was cool her before lying down on the sun mattress.

I picked up her discarded clothes from the hall and put them in the bedroom. I peeled off my own clothes, wrapped a towel round my waist and went into the kitchen, where I loaded Martini fixings on to a tray.

The ice was so cold it crackled in the jug.

I took the tray and an old silk dressing gown of mine out to Daisy on the balcony.

Don't tell me, I said. You just can't wait to get your hands on my body.

Daisy closed her eyes and smiled.

I was so hot, she said. I thought I would die. I thought my teeth would melt.

I sat next to her on the sun mattress.

Oh well, I said. Maybe later. I brought you this in case you burn.

I covered her with my dressing gown.

Shove over, I said.

She moved to the edge of the mattress and I lay down beside her.

Drink? I said.

Mm, she said, her eyes closed. Mm. Lovely.

You don't really have to go to work, do you? I said. Not really. Not yet.

She turned over on to her side. Her breath tickled my face.

Not really, she said. Not yet.

That's good, I said.

I lay back and closed my eyes.

The slam of a door woke me. I was lying on my back covered with my dressing gown and the sun was level with the treetops. I sat up and swallowed. I was alone. I swallowed again. The Martini fixings were still on their tray, the jug half filled with melted ice. I stood up and put on my dressing gown.

Daisy, I said. Daisy.

She didn't answer. I picked up the tray and took it through into the kitchen.

I called Daisy again. She still didn't answer. I figured she'd probably decided to go and do some work after all, but thought I'd have a look through the flat anyway.

I reached the bedroom before I noticed that all her things were gone.

I checked and checked again. Her clothes had gone. Her make-up had gone. The radio and the pot had gone. I spent a long time going from room to room, checking.

Then I cleaned the kitchen. I couldn't think of anything else to do.

I washed everything up. I put everything away.

I wiped surfaces and cleaned the sink.

I washed the hob and took all the food out of the fridge ready to defrost it.

I mopped the floor and cleaned the oven and mopped the floor round the oven again.

Then I moved on to the bathroom. There wasn't much to do in there.

Daisy usually kept all that pretty clean.

I swept the balcony.

I vacuumed the hall.

I dusted and tidied the drawing room. I took the cushions off the chairs and hoovered down the back of the sofa.

I made a pile of old magazines and threw them in the bin.

I didn't find anything of Daisy's anywhere.

Nothing.

I left the bedroom until last. I changed the sheets and pillow-cases. I turned the mattress. I went through the drawers and cupboards. She'd been thorough, I'll say that for her.

She did make one slip up though. On the bedside table, still under the glass where she'd left it, I found the note she'd left me on the morning after Jack's party.

The day before yesterday.

So I had something to remember her by after all.

I sat on the edge of the bed, holding the note, and remembered her.

I sort of half thought she might call. I folded the note and put it in the drawer of the bedside table. I sat and looked at the phone for a long time, but of course she didn't call.

You don't go round someone's flat minutely removing every trace of your presence if you're going to call.

What was there to say anyway?

When I was through looking at the telephone, I looked at the television. I flipped through the channels but there wasn't anything on, so I switched it off and looked at the blank screen.

I mean, what do you do?

I went to bed.

I like to sleep on my right side, but I couldn't because of my ear and my swollen face which throbbed as soon as I brought it near the pillow, so I lay on my back and waited for sleep.

It was a long time coming.

I woke up with the left side of my face buried in the pillow, deaf to everything but the surge of blood in my head and with my right eye gummed shut.

Stiffly I turned on to my back and lifted my head.

The room had gone into white shift.

At the foot of the bed, perched on the rail, was the white peacock.

Head under wing.

Its tail a river of white hanging down to the floor.

I sat up. The jolt of the bed disturbed the peacock, it shifted its feet on the rail and brought its head out from under its wing. It looked around. It stretched its legs. It stretched first one wing then the other. It rustled its shimmering tail. Then it tucked its head under its wing again, settled down again on the bedrail and went back to sleep.

FOUR

For everything that happens to you there is a day when it has not happened and a day when it has. You spend deserts of time brooding on this. Why, only yesterday . . . you think. Only this time last week . . . Happier times . . . you think. One day here, one day gone. This cannot have happened. I mean, here I am, just carrying on after yesterday. Life continues its quotidian pattern. The same things have to be done as had to be done yesterday. There are the same advertisements on the television as there were yesterday, when I was happy. There is one particular advertisement I shall never be able to see again without remembering the Sunday after Daisy left me. That really makes my whites white, the woman said, looking at the same time forthright and relieved, for all the world as if nothing had ever changed, as if my life was not ever going to change, as if Daisy had just slipped out for a while to fix up a few last-minute details with Mason, whoever Mason was, and would be back in a minute to kick off her shoes, let down her hair, demand a cup of tea and smile at me. How can this be? I thought. How can everything be so ordinary. Why, only yesterday . . . And your head goes round and round thinking about it. All the time you're not saying Why? or How could she? you're thinking about it. One day here, one day gone. And it hurts, thinking about it, so you banish it from your mind. But you quickly realize that that's a mistake, because it brings you right up face to face with an insuperable problem: What are you going to do? I don't mean, what are you going to do about it? I mean, what are you actually going to do? How are you going to pass all that time? All those blank hours to spend, you might as well spend them brooding as anything else.

I woke up late. Feeling, I have to say, a lot better. Which wasn't the boon it might have been, because if I'd felt lousy at least I could have stayed in bed and moped and fussed. As it was, I felt rested and fresh. My body, although the mirror showed no appreciable difference, was unstiff.

I had a bath and sponged my wounded eye open. As I ducked my head under the water to wet my hair my ear opened. It bubbled and popped and rushed and I could hear again.

I spun the bath out for as long as I could. I shampooed my hair twice, a thing I never usually do, and when I'd finished and put on the old silk dressing gown I'd used to cover Daisy yesterday, I carefully cleaned the tub and tidied the room. I was as thorough as I could be, but even so I only managed to take thirty-five minutes, so I went to see if I could do anything in the kitchen.

There I found all the stuff I'd taken out of the fridge to defrost it. So I spent a further half hour swabbing down the fridge, rinsing it out with lemon juice, washing all the trays and loading it back up again.

I ate. I couldn't stop eating. I ate two apples, some digestive biscuits, half a packet of peppermints, a bacon sandwich, and a pot of chocolate mousse that had been sitting in the fridge since the pre-Daisy days. I made a pot of tea and let it go cold while I ate a bowl of muesli, a packet of crinkle-cut chips, a salami sandwich, the remains of a bowl of peach and greengage compôte, and the contents of the cheese bell (a heel of Derby Sage, some Dolcelatte, and a dry fragment of blue Brie). I made another pot of tea and went to the bedroom. There wasn't much to do there, but as I was making the bed I remembered the peacock.

The white peacock sitting on my bedrail in the middle of the night.

That couldn't be right.

I mean, for a start, how did it get there? Even if it had come in through the bedroom window, how had it reached it? Even if I'd left open the bedroom, the drawing room, and the balcony doors, and I couldn't say I hadn't, there was the problem of how it could have got on to the balcony.

I went out to see how far away the nearest tree was. It was a good thirty yards, more if you measured from the nearest peacock-bearing branch. Peacocks could fly, I knew. But there's a difference between flying up to a lowhanging branch to roost on it and flying thirty yards over to my balcony from a tree they'd have to flap like hell to get to the top of, which was a couple of hundred yards at least from their roosting place. It didn't seem possible to me.

And yet the peacock had been there.

I decided that the only thing to do was to go across to the park and see if I could find a keeper or someone who could tell me how far a peacock can fly. And if they could fly a reasonable distance, there was the problem solved.

I had trouble getting out of the flat. I got dressed quickly enough. I just chucked on a T-shirt, jeans and sneakers. But I had trouble leaving.

I went through the old ritual. I shut the windows. I checked that the oven was turned off. I unplugged the television and turned off the immersion heater. But at the door I couldn't remember if I'd done it all and had to go and check again. At the door a second time I couldn't remember having turned off the immersion heater and had to go and look yet again. Half-way down the stairs I found I'd forgotten my wallet so I went back to fetch it. Half-way down the stairs a second time I heard the telephone ring and raced back to answer it.

I dropped the key at the door and my hand was shaking so much that I had a hard time getting it into the lock. I was pretty out of breath by the time I got to the phone.

Hello, I said.

Hello, a voice said.

Not Daisy's.

I panted.

Hello, the voice said.

A man's voice.

Hello? Peter-Patrick?

Hi, I said.

Hello, the voice said. O'Brien here.

Grey-flannels' voice.

Oh hi, I said. how are you? I was just on my way out. Good to hear from you.

Yes, he said. Good to hear you too. Listen. I have some news for you. It's Mason. We've wangled it.

Ah, I said.

There was never much doubt really, he said. Not after he saw you. Nice party, by the way, wasn't it?

Great, I said.

Well, anyway, he said. He saw you, and he liked you and he wants you to drop over today for a few formalities.

Ah, I said.

Nothing much, he said. Just a few last-minute details.

Listen, I said. Look. I'm not quite sure . . . I don't know . . . What are we talking about?

Grey-flannels laughed.

You don't know? he said. Daisy didn't tell you? You actually don't know?

I don't know, I said.

Well, he said. That's a good one. That Daisy, she's the best.

Daisy isn't here, I said. She's gone away.

And she didn't tell you, he said. That is a good one.

No, I said. She didn't tell me. What didn't she tell me?

About Mason, he said.

Mason? I said.

Mason, he said. Philip Mason.

It hit me.

Philip Mason.

Philip Mason!

I went hot and cold.

114

No, I said. She didn't tell me.

Well anyway, he said. He wants you. He's doing this series. He thinks you'd be great in the part. He wants you.

What series? I said.

Hang on, he said. Wait a bit. Ah yes. The Chronicles of Carlingford. Whatever they may be. Eleven one-hour episodes, and a two-hour episode at the beginning and end. Some Victorian epic or other. You are someone called the Reverend Frank Wentworth.

Look, I said. I've had this accident. I look a bit rough. My face is a mess, frankly.

Ah, he said. Well. We'll have to hope he won't worry too much about that. Not now he's seen you. I mean, it's nothing permanent, I hope.

So do I, I said.

Just you get on over there, he said. He's at the Savoy. I told him you'd be round after lunch.

Well, I said. Yes. Well. What can I say? Yes.

I'll get round there right away. Thanks.

Don't thank me, he said. Thank Daisy. She did most of the arranging. I was just there as a front.

Well, thanks anyway, I said. For being a front.

That Daisy, he said. What a woman. And she didn't even tell you.

Yes, I said. She's quite a woman.

Give her my love, Grey-flannels said.

I will, I said. I will. When I see her.

We hung up.

I changed.

For Philip Mason you change.

For Philip Mason you do the whole bit.

I pressed my navy blue blazer and a pair of sand-coloured needlecords. I wore them with a stripy Paul Smith shirt and a blue and white polka dot cravat. Tan shoes and matching argyle socks.

I called a taxi and went down to wait for it on the street.

When it arrived I was just about to get in when it occurred to me that I couldn't remember turning off the iron.

I told the driver to hang on and went back up to check. On the way back up I thought, Don't be silly. Of course you turned it off. You always turn it off. You turn it off, you wrap the flex round the base and leave it on a tile in the kitchen to cool. It's what you always do.

I went back down to the taxi. At the front door I thought, Just because you always do it doesn't mean you've done it now. You ought to go and look.

I put the key in the door to open it again.

I took the key out.

I put it back in again and opened the door.

Jesus, I thought. Jesus, this is ridiculous. This has got to stop.